Dream Reaper
AND OTHER TALES FROM THE MULTIVERSE

MJ Carambat

Dream Reaper
And Other Tales From the Multiverse

Copyright © 2013 by MJ Carambat

ISBN: 978-0-9912468-1-6

Printed in the United States of America

November 2013

Table of Contents

Foreword

The multiverse is an amazing concept, isn't it? An infinite stack of universes, all existing at the same time and place, just in different states of probability through time. Many of these worlds are nearly identical to the subatomic level, yet some are vastly different.

Whether you realize it or not, you're a traveller between these worlds. You do it every day. You make the jump with every decision you make, and every whim of chance. You leave behind your family and friends, jumping into an exciting new universe with every right turn or left turn, only to meet nearly identical quantum copies of them with every leap. Most people never notice the millions of jumps they make every day, except for the odd phenomenon of deja vu, or when buildings or trees suddenly show up when you could have sworn they weren't there before.

These stories are snapshots—adventures and interpretations of humanity across the multiverse. Like you, they have traversed the gap between worlds and made their way to this reality. I hope you enjoy them as much as I enjoyed writing them down.

- MJ Carambat

2

Dream Reaper

Emmie, alone in the woods—*again.*

The impossibly high trees, barely visible in the dim light of the lesser of Terser's two moons always made the frightened little girl feel smaller than she already was. The impassive lunar crescent was the only source of light in this dark and fearful place. She shivered beneath her thin, pink nightgown and wished hopelessly for her mommy.

Her tummy felt sick. She knew what was coming...what was coming *for her.* Her heart beat rapidly and she tried not to cry, knowing her sobs would only bring it faster, but there was nothing she could do. No one would hear her screams in this place. No one ever did.

Hearing a rustle in the bushes, the little girl took a step backwards. A horrible, chittering sound followed it, a sound she knew well. Desperate for it to go away, she closed her eyes and moved to cover her ears, but unexpectedly found a stuffed bear grasped in her tiny hand. She hugged Mr. Warbles tightly, grateful for the company, but he'd never made an appearance before. *How had he gotten here?*

Warbles stared at her blankly, his bad eye drooping where the stitching had come loose. If he had any answers, he wasn't telling.

"Are you here to protect me?" she asked the bear. Its head lolled to one side as if asleep. Emmie shook it violently. "Wake up Warbles! We need to wake up!"

The chittering became louder—an insect-like buzzing overlaid with a strange whispering voice she couldn't understand. Emmie spun around in a panic, but saw nothing. It seemed to be coming from everywhere. Her already rapid heartbeat pumped even faster in her small chest. Her eyes went wide with fright.

Long, thin, tentacle-like shadows reached towards her from behind the trees, creeping slowly, writhing along the ground like twisting snakes. She recoiled in horror, but they were everywhere. A shadow touched her ankle, burning her as if stabbed by a hot knife. Emmie screamed in pain and ran, dropping Mr. Warbles in a pile of dank, moss covered leaves as she fled into the woods.

* * *

"It's okay Emmie sweetie, mama's here," soothed Elise Lawson, as she rocked the five year old in her lap. Her little girl was sobbing inconsolably after having another one of her nightmares. "It was just a dream. You're safe. Everything's going to be alright."

Emmie stirred and Elise brushed a leaf out of her daughter's long brown hair. *How had that gotten there?* The questions would have to wait till morning, the poor girl was upset and her eyes were bloodshot with lack of sleep. Elise was nearly as tired herself. She was up with Emmie almost every night now. She whispered a nursery rhyme in her ear and the wails slowed to a few hiccupping sobs.

Amanda, Emmie's older sister, peered down from the upper bunk. "Shut it already, Emmie! Mama, make her go back to sleep." The fifteen-year-old shared the room with her younger sibling, a situation she was not particularly fond of.

Elise frowned. "That's enough, Amanda. She's only five. You've had a few nightmares yourself."

"Not as many as her. She's just doing it for attention," said the teenager.

Hearing her older sister's voice, Emmie turned to her and asked, "Da da...do you have Mr. Warbles?"

"No, I don't have your stupid bear. Stop bothering everyone and go back to sleep." Amanda turned over and pulled her pillow over her head.

"Mama…I think I left him there," said Emmie, her face turning pale. "I left Warbles in the woods. Poor Mr. Warbles."

"What woods, sweet heart? Warbles went to be bed with you tonight. He's probably just hiding under the covers." Elise pulled back the sheets on Emmie's bed. *Where was that bear?* It was going to be hard enough to get her back to sleep as it was, but without Warbles it would be nearly impossible. She pulled them back further, but only uncovered a small pile of leaves and twigs.

"Emmie honey, where did all this come from?" asked her mother, scooping the decaying debris into a wastebasket.

Emmie buried her head in her mother's shoulder and whimpered. "I want Mr. Warbles!"

Elise turned on the light and started searching the room. Amanda sat up and rolled her eyes. "Really mama? Really? Why do you always do what she wants? It's like I don't even exist. I hate her." She shoved the pillow back over her head.

Elise sighed. She regretted having kids so many years apart. The teenager had little in common with her much younger sister. Worse, Amanda held her to the same standards as herself and they were always fighting.

"Emmie sweetie, you can come sleep with mama tonight, okay? We'll find Mr. Warbles in the morning."

The shaken little girl nodded and Elise picked her up. Giving Amanda a peck on the cheek, Elise turned out the light and carried Emmie to her bedroom down the hall. It was going to be another long night.

* * *

"The Tersians invited us to come here, Nick. I don't see where there's a problem," said Elise into the videx as she sipped her morning coffee. The reception was horrible and she could barely make out her ex-husband's angry face.

They were having the same old argument, the one Nick refused to drop; another annoying attempt in a long list of ploys to get them to return to Earth. The controlling jerk simply couldn't come to terms with her leaving him and moving off-world.

"But the recent deaths! You can't tell me it's not dangerous there," said Nick. "Three children brutally slaughtered in their hammocks. Two others, gone missing. Of course I'm worried. You need to come back to Earth."

Elise knew how gruesome the murders were. The parents had found what was left of their children in the morning. Their clothing was ripped to shreds, soaked in blood. Eviscerated from throat to waist, parts of their bodies looked eaten away or torn off.

Frightening as it was, Elise had weighed the risks and decided to stay. After all, the murderer was targeting Tersians, not humans. This was an internal problem and had nothing to do with them. It would take a lot more than this to force her family back to Earth.

"The Tersians are dealing with it. It's got nothing to do with us. We're still their guests," said Elise. "This colony is an amazing opportunity for me, Nick. The biodiversity on this planet is stunning. You can't expect me to drop all my work simply because some Tersian has gone berserk. They'll catch the lunatic. Don't worry."

"From what I hear, they're *blaming* the humans. They say the trouble started when you and the other colonists landed. They're saying it's some kind of pissed off demon. The only reason you aren't being pushed off world is because they need our med tech so badly."

"Nick, there's no such thing as ghosts and demons. Yes, the disease they are facing is strange and complex. Our technology is helping the symptoms but we still don't know what the cause is. It doesn't seem to be viral or bacterial, it's something else entirely. This is why my research is so important."

"Damn your research, Elise! You should realize that things don't always fit into your little world of precise weights and measurements. Sometimes, you just need to trust your gut," said her ex-husband. "I don't know if those superstitious primitives are right or not, but I do know that Tersians are incredibly passive and peaceful. Crime among the tribes is almost unheard of. I can't see any of them killing one another."

"I'm sorry Nick, but there is a rational explanation for all this. The authorities are looking into it. If it makes you feel any better, I'll lock the girl's room tonight. I think Emmie might be walking in her sleep and I certainly don't want her going outside again."

"What makes you think she's sleep walking?" asked Nick concerned.

"Last night I found a pile of leaves in her bed. I think she might have gone into the front courtyard for some reason."

Nick's eyes went wide. "Elise! This is serious! How long has she been doing this? Are you telling me our five-year-old went outside into the night all by herself with a murderer on the loose?"

"Calm down, Nick. I don't know what she did. The door alarm was set, but it didn't go off for some reason. I'm having it checked out. There aren't any windows in the kid's room, and I'm putting a lock on her door. She'll be fine."

"You're putting the kids in jeopardy, Elise. You and your pointless research. Someday you'll realize what's important in life, hopefully before you lose it." Nick clicked the videx off abruptly and his scowling image faded.

Elise considered the conversation a moment longer, tapping her fingers on the table. *No, there wasn't any danger. Nick was just overreacting as usual. This had nothing to do with the humans...and certainly, nothing to do with demons.*

* * *

Elise woke to the frantic screams of her daughter. Instantly awake, she threw off the covers and sat bolt upright. This wasn't the quiet sobbing from the nightmares, it sounded like Emmie was being attacked.

Stumbling in the dark, she painfully rammed her thigh into the nightstand. A lamp fell over with a crash. Wincing, she limped down the hall to her daughter's room, trying to avoid stepping on broken glass.

"Emmie! Emmie! What's going on? I'm coming!"

As her daughter wailed, she could hear strange clicking and whispering noises coming from inside the room. She fumbled with the doorknob, but the door wouldn't open. Cursing, she remembered the new lock. She pushed on the latch, but it refused to budge. Somehow, the new lock was rusted shut. She banged her fists again the stubborn iron bar.

"Mama! Mama!" Emmie screamed.

Elise threw herself against the wooden door. She tried again, and again...nothing. Her shoulder throbbed as she stepped back for another barrage. Long black tendrils of nothingness coiled around the edges of the door. Elise gasped.

Were those shadows? Or worse...smoke? Was there a fire in the girl's room? She put her hand on the door, but it wasn't hot at all—actually, it was freezing.

She suddenly realized that Emmie had stopped screaming.

In a panic, she banged on the door. "Emmie! Amanda! What's going on in there?"

The shadowy tentacles slowly withdrew back inside the room and the door shuddered. She heard a skittering, scratching sound, as if something was dragging a large, sharp-clawed animal away against its will.

Grabbing the first large thing she could find, Elise overturned a plaster pedestal, knocking a potted plant to the floor. Slamming the makeshift battering ram into the door, the latch broke free and clattered to the floor. Panting heavily, she shoved the door open.

Stepped into the room, she felt the cold beneath her bare feet. Except for the soft glow of a few bulbsticks that Amanda liked to keep burning, the room was dark and eerily silent. She turned on the light, afraid of what she'd see.

Catching her breath in disbelief, she found the room filled with wet, decaying leaves and muck.

A radiating explosion of foul-smelling foliage completely covered the children's bunk bed, floor and most of the walls and ceiling. Long, deep gouges scored the plaster walls and ceiling as if someone had let an ape lose in the room with a chain saw. She scanned the ruined room for her missing children.

She found Emmie sitting in the center of her bed, with her head down, in some sort of trance. Her lips were moving as if speaking, but there was no sound. She was soaking wet and mud stained her nightgown.

She grabbed her by the shoulders and tried to snap her out of it, shaking her cold, light frame. Her blue lips continued to mouth barely audible, unfamiliar words. "Emmie, what's happened? Where's Amanda?"

Not getting an answer, she tilted Emmie's head back to meet her gaze, and saw black, unseeing orbs instead of her daughter's beautiful green eyes. "Oh my God Emmie. What's wrong with your eyes?"

Not knowing what else to do, she picked her little girl up and tried to warm her. As she rubbed her arms and legs, the frightful black eyes slowly faded back to normal and the little girl became more responsive, although she was obviously exhausted. Elise tearfully begged her to speak,

"Please baby, where's Amanda? What happened?"

Emmie half-opened one eye and coarsely whispered, "Did it go back home, Mama?"

"Did what go back home, sweetie? For God's sake, tell me what's going on!" Elise was nearly hysterical as she tried to keep her daughter from falling unconscious. Her efforts proved useless; there was nothing she could do. She was only able to get two more words out of her before she fell into a deep sleep.

"The demon..."

* * *

"And the child hasn't spoken to anyone since?" asked Inspector Lamez, verifying the notes on his videx. Elise rubbed her tired eyes and looked away. "I'm sorry Ms. Lawson, I know this is hard for you, but I need to know what happened here."

She turned to the detective and glared at him. "Hard for me? Don't make me laugh! You haven't any idea of what I'm going through. My daughter's gone missing, poor Emmie's been traumatized and a forest has appeared in my children's room. No Inspector, I don't think you have any idea of how hard this is for me."

Nevertheless, Lamez continued his inquiry. "About the debris you found. Why did you have it removed before the official investigation began?"

"Because I needed to find my daughter. I did not intend to wait 72 hours for Planetary Security to decide my Amanda hadn't just run away. My team collected the debris the night Amanda disappeared. We've been looking for answers, but keep finding more questions."

"You mentioned your youngest said something about a demon. Have you found anything to support that claim? Maybe something in the debris?"

Elise looked at the chrono on her videx. She needed to wrap this up and get back to the lab. "Not much, except that the leaves and branches are very unusual. Although they are Tersian, they're from prehistoric trees, which no longer exist. There's another thing too. There's something odd about the amount we collected. It's roughly equivalent to the mass of my daughter."

"Surely, that's just a coincidence," said the Inspector.

"At first, I thought so as well, but then I remembered Mr. Warbles."

"Mr. Warbles?" asked Lamez, flipping back a few pages on his videx to review his notes.

"Yes, my daughter's teddy bear. He went missing the night before, and I remembered that there was a teddy-sized pile of leaves left behind," said Elise.

"That's very interesting. The two events might be related. If you don't mind, I'll stop by your lab after my forensic team finishes in the girl's room." said Lamez. "Any idea on how the girls might have gotten out?"

"I can't explain it. I had the door bolted from the outside. I thought maybe Ellie was sleepwalking and I didn't want her leaving. I can only assume someone got into the house and broke into their room. For some reason, they took—" Elise's voice cracked at the mention of her missing daughter. "They took Amanda, but left Emmie behind."

Mercifully, Lamez put away his videx and ended the interview. "I think that's all I need for now Ms. Lawson. Thank you for your time. Please know, I'm going to do all I can to find your daughter."

His reassurances didn't make her feel any better. Instead, the interview had made her feel worse. The inquiry made her relive the horrors of that night. She didn't want to remember that she had heard noises in the girl's room—hideous, chattering noises. She didn't want to remember that cold presence of evil and how every bone in her body wanted her to run screaming out of her house.

An hour later, Elise pulled into the hover lot outside the outpost research facility. As a scientist, she would focus on her daughter's disappearance as a problem to research and solve. There were clues to follow, and she was certain she would find a logical explanation—*an explanation that didn't involve the paranormal.*

* * *

"[kik] [shreez] [kik] [kik]?" inquired the Tersian boy, poking the sleeping Earthie with the tip of an arrow.

"Wha...?" Amanda replied, still groggy from sleep. She felt cold, wet, and stiff all over, and someone was jabbing her side. She turned and opened her eyes.

The oddly proportioned, large-eyed face of a Tersian youth came closely into focus, making her jump back. The movement hurt a lot. Her whole body hurt. She rubbed some warmth into her arms, and looked confusedly at her tormentor. He returned the arrow to his quiver and stared back at her bemused. She always thought Tersians looked like almond-eyed space elves, but until now she had never met one her own age. He was actually kind of cute.

"Who are you? What are you doing in my…" she wanted to say *bedroom,* but was surprised to find she wasn't in it anymore. Instead of the light pink, unicorn adorned walls of her room, thin, pale trees stretched into the sky all around her. She was in a dark forest with trees that so tall she wasn't able to see the tops.

"[kik] [kik]," said the boy, smiling. He offered his hand to help her out of the pile of stinking leaves she was lying in.

"What the frick? How did I get here? Where am I?" demanded Amanda, still suspicious of the youth, but taking his hand anyway. He was surprisingly strong, considering his lithe frame. She shyly took a step or two away from him and wiped some of the dirt off herself.

The boy cleared his throat, and said slowly, "Ters…za…day…shuh." Then, with a little more confidence, he continued, "You zin Tersedasia."

Amanda was impressed. She hadn't expected him to answer in English. Although, most Tersians could understand their language, many had trouble putting the right sounds together to speak actual words. Normally, the natives communicated with a series of gestures, guttural clicks and whistles.

"Tersedasia? How is that possible? Did you bring me here?" she asked.

"No. You bringed yourself," said the youth, getting a better handle on the language, but still frowning. He seemed confused about her being here. "Zis *Tersian* dream place. Earthies not come here."

Amanda had heard about the strange place Tersians went to when they dreamed. Researchers in Tersian biology, like her mother, simply assumed it was a deeply embedded racial memory from their ancient past, which they all shared. They also discovered that unlike humans, Tersians were unable to wake themselves if they were threatened in their dreams. Occasionally, they could even die in their sleep. Amanda wondered what would happen if *she* died here.

"This is the dream place? Well, it seems pretty real to me, and pretty frickin' cold." said Amanda, shivering. "But ok, I get it. So you're saying I'm dreaming?"

The boy smiled and shrugged. Apparently, he wasn't so sure.

Somewhere a twig snapped and the boy lost his
smile. He reached for her and suggested they
hide deeper in the woods. She timidly took his
hand and let him lead the way. Hurrying along
paths only the boy could see, she learned his
name was Namu. He wasn't able to pronounce
hers, instead calling her something like 'Da na da'
which made her think of her sister.

"Have you seen another human here? A little
one? My sister, Emmie?" she asked her new
friend.

"Sister? No. Only you, me and—"

A strange insect-like noise cut him off. He cocked
his head to one side, listening for more of the
chittering whispers, warning her not to move.
Quietly unslinging his bow, he fit an arrow to it.
After a few minutes, the sound repeated, only
this time, it was more distant.

"What was that?" asked Amanda. The sound had
sent chills up her spine.

"Demon," said Namu. "Dream place not safe
anymore for Tersians."

"What about for Earthies?"

Namu looked at her concerned. He pointed at the
softly glowing horizon. "Tersians leave

Tersedasia when sun comes. Earthies…I think, not."

"You're leaving me here alone, then?" asked Amanda, fear rising. Surely, she would wake up soon, and this would all be over.

He looked at her sadly. "Meet here again tonight. Hide. Keep safe."

Amanda watched the sunrise between the trees. The sun looked huge on the horizon, casting impossibly long shadows through the woods. As the light increased, vibrantly colored flowers filled the previously dismal forest. She wondered why it looked so different and foreboding at night. She turned to ask Namu, but he had already disappeared.

* * *

Another wasted day with no answers. Elise stared at her bedroom ceiling unable to sleep. The debris wasn't telling them anything else and neither was Emmie. Planetary Security had hoped their specialist in child psychology would get something out of her, but they hadn't been successful either.

Even though Lamaz put a security detail outside, there was no way Elise was letting her little girl out of her sight. The five-year-old slept fitfully next to her, with her back turned. *Why wouldn't she talk? What had happened that night?* Often, she begged and pleaded with Emmie to tell her, but she would just start crying. At times she felt like grabbing the frustrating child and shaking the words out of her, but what good would that do? Emmie would speak when she was ready; no one could make her. Until then, Elise was doing everything possible to find Amanda.

Emmie pulled herself into a ball as a chill ran through the room. It was really getting cold now; the room felt like a refrigerator. Elise pulled the covers up over both their shoulders and shivered under the covers. She hugged her little girl close and quietly sang in her ear.

The little girl turned sleepily towards her mother, with her head down and whispered something unintelligible, her breath forming a light haze in the cold gloom of Elise's bedroom. Surprised and hopeful, Elise drew her face closer, "Did you say something, sweetheart?"

Emmie's head snapped up so suddenly, that Elise recoiled in shocked surprise. She put a hand over her mouth to stifle a scream as Emmie stared at her, staring with cold, pitch-black eyes. Heart pounding, she watched as her daughter sat up and pointed, terrified at something only she could see at the foot of the bed.

Elise looked where she pointed, but saw only shadows. "Emmie! What is it? I don't see…"

Elise blinked and the room changed. One moment they were in her bedroom, and in the next she was in some sort of dark forest. She could hear the animal noises from before—a chittering, whispering clatter coming from all around them. But this time she could *feel* something's presence, a presence she now oddly recognized. It was something from her childhood, something so evil that it shouldn't exist, something she had tried hard to forget. A familiar cold, primal fear gripped her and more than anything she wanted to run, but she had to protect her daughter.

She tried to find Emmie, but the world was in chaos, constantly flickering back and forth like a candle's changing shadows. In some places, Elise could see both worlds superimposed over each other like a double exposure. The chittering and whispering got louder. She screamed for her daughter over the tumult.

Emmie was backing away on all fours from sinister shadows creeping towards her over the leaves. Elise couldn't be sure of anything. At first, Ellie was backed against a stark tree, a second later she was pinned against the bedroom wall. In a scene that made her skin crawl, she watched in horrified fascination, as Emmie appeared to scale the smooth wall towards the ceiling like a four-legged spider. Once there, she continued across it, sticking to it upside-down like an enormous fly.

"Mama! Mama! Help me," she screamed down to her.

The scene flickered and they were back in the forest. Emmie cowered in a branch a few feet above her head. It shook violently as something invisible, but powerful, swiped at the tree's base, gouging deep grooves in its rough hexagonal bark pattern. Elise collapsed to her knees. How could she go through this again? She had already lost one daughter, and was about to lose another. What could she could do? Nothing made sense. There was no order here, only fear. So much fear she couldn't think—fear of the present and fear of the past. A horrible and tragic memory had surfaced, and it had frozen her to the spot.

Something sizzled past her ear. The creature screamed in rage as an arrow embedded itself in its flank and the demon flickered into view. Elise could see it's enormously powerful body, row after row of razor sharp teeth, and glowing red eyes. All four of them stared at her with intense hatred.

A large rock bounced off the demon's horned head, followed by two more arrows. It screamed in pain and took a step back. Another rock found its mark, catching it squarely between its upper set of eyes. The demon staggered for a moment, regained its balance, and howled in rage, shaking the forest with the sound.

The demon charged her, horns lowered. Another arrow caught it squarely in the chest, but it barely affected the enraged beast. Unable to move, Elise closed her eyes and prepared to die. The thunderous approach of the demon grew louder and louder but instead of ending in her bloody death there was only silence. A cheer went up behind her.

Elise turned and opened her eyes. Silhouetted in the light of the morning sun, two youths approached her. One was a Tersian boy, carrying a bow and arrow, but the other was…

"Amanda!" Elise shouted, rising to meet her.

Amanda dropped the large rock she was carrying and hugged her mother. "Mama! Emmie! You're both here! I don't believe it!"

Emmie climbed out of the tree and ran to her sister. "Da da! Da da!"

"I found your stupid bear," said Amanda, reaching behind her back. She brought out a very dirty Mr. Warbles and handed it to her sister.

Emmie squealed with delight and hugged her sister.

* * *

Through tear-stained eyes, Elise held her children as the sun slowly rose, filling the woods with a warm, golden light. She shook with relief. Somehow, they were all still alive, and the evil presence was gone. Although, she doubted something as insignificant as a few arrows and rocks had anything to do with it.

"Amanda, what happened to that monster, and where's your friend?" asked Elise, wanting to thank the young Tersian.

"It's not gone. It'll be back," said Amanda unhappily. "Like Namu, the demon is forced out when the sun comes up. They'll both be back later tonight. You were very lucky the sun rose when it did. That thing almost squished you. Why didn't you run when we were distracting it?"

"I...I..." started her mother, unable to tell her the terrible truth. She couldn't explain to her teenaged daughter what even now was filling her with a paralyzing fear. Guilt, tragedy and loss flooded into her soul as memory after memory flowed back. She changed the subject. "Tersedasia? Is that where this is?"

"Yes. It's the place Tersians go when they dream," said Amanda. "By the way, I'd really like to wake up now. Am I still in my bed? Are you asleep too?"

Elise looked at her quizzically. "Sweetheart, I don't think either of us are sleeping right now. You went missing two days ago. I don't exactly know how, but I think we're actually here."

Emmie tugged at her mother's hem. "Mama, Mama. I know! I know! It's like a seesaw."

"What's she talking about now?" asked Amanda. "I just want to go home."

"Seesaw, Da da! Seesaw!" said Emmie. "You press down on one side, and the other side goes up. It's easy."

Elise knew all too well what she was talking about. The memory of it now burned crisply in her mind. She couldn't have been much older than Emmie when she discovered what she could do. She had done something so horrible with her gift that she had hidden it from herself her entire life. Now, it had finally caught up with her.

She sat down on a fallen tree and pulled her oldest aside. "Amanda, your sister is...well, your sister is *special.*"

"Yeah, like in special *ed,*" said Amanda.

"No. I'm serious. She's got a very unusual gift. Something she's too young to fully understand. You're not going to believe this, but Emmie can bring things in and out of her dreams, including *people.*"

Amanda stared at her mother open mouthed. "You're kidding me, right? Tell me you're not serious."

"Do you remember the little pile of leaves the night Mr. Warbles went missing?"

"Yeah, what about it?"

"Well, that's how it works. Remember conservation of mass and energy from your science class? You can neither destroy nor create mass or energy. So when something from our world enters another, an exchange must take place. That's Emmie's seesaw."

"So why did the twerp send me here?" she asked.

"She was probably just scared and wanted you with her. You've got to remember, she's been coming here for weeks, facing that demon all alone. I think it forced her abilities to the surface."

"Lucky for her she's an Earthie. Tersians can't wake up when they're threatened. They're stuck here in the woods until the sun comes up," said Amanda. "Namu says that's why all those kids have died. When they die here, they die in real life as well."

Elise had wondered why the kids displayed the physical symptoms of being attacked. She thought maybe it was some sort of extreme psychosomatic reaction, but considering the extent of their injuries, that sounded ludicrous. Really, after what she had seen and felt here, she was ready to believe the paranormal might have more to do with it than science.

"So, why is she dreaming of Tersedasia like a Tersian? What happens when she wakes up?" asked Amanda.

"I don't know," said Elise, who was wondering much the same thing. "Any idea where the demon came from?"

"Namu says it's a demon from an ancient legend. They call them *Dream Reapers.* He said before there were people, demons roamed their planet. Some of them lived forever and never died. When Namu's people appeared, they fought the monsters, drove them into the sky, and sealed them away. However, sometimes they try to return through their dreams when the world is weak."

"And now they think the world is weak because of the disease?" asked Elise.

"Yeah, that's most of it, but also because of us. They appreciate us, but think that asking for our help was a sign of weakness. Now the Reaper is bent on destroying them all."

Elise had a theory. If she was right, it would explain everything: the disease, Tersedasia, the Reaper, the murdered kids...everything. A bold plan formed in her mind, but what she needed to do frightened her. She needed to talk with Inspector Lamez as soon as possible. With his help, she might be able to put an end to it.

"Emmie honey. Can you send us back home?" she asked.

Emmie shook her head and clung to her mother's leg. "Don't wanna! It's scary here."

"Don't worry sweetheart. I'll wake you up when we get back. You won't be here alone anymore."

"Promise?"

"Yes. I promise. Oh, and we won't forget Mr. Warbles this time." Elise took the bear from her, and waved one of his paws at her nose.

Emmie giggled and said, "Ok, mama. Hold Da da's hand and close your eyes."

Elise felt a disorienting sideways motion as the ground beneath her jerked. When she opened her eyes, she was standing in her bedroom, holding Amanda in one hand, and Mr. Warbles in the other. The room smelled of the old leaves that had probably been in the room when she went over, but had since returned. An Amanda-sized dresser was now missing, as was most of the clothing inside it. *Conversation of mass and energy,* she marveled. *Some laws are unbreakable even with the paranormal.*

She found Emmie asleep on the bed, sleeping soundly. She was tempted not to wake her, but remembered her promise. Elise shook her lightly and kissed her cheek, and she sleepily opened her eyes—her perfectly normal, beautiful green eyes.

* * *

"So basically, you want me to arrest a nightmare," said Inspector Lamez, casually stirring his coffee. "I mean, that's what you're telling me, right Ms. Lawson?"

Elise frowned and crossed her arms. Lamez still didn't believe her. "Look, when you get there you can put cuffs on it and read it its rights or whatever else you'd like to do with it. Personally, I'd prefer you laser it into hamburger. I've seen this thing, and it's not something you want to mess with."

"Actually, I saw what was left of your bedroom, and after reading the security detail's report, I'm inclined to agree with your assessment of the animal," said the Inspector, taking a sip of his coffee.

"It's not an animal, Inspector Lamez. I've explained this. It's something far worse."

"Oh yes... it's a *dream demon*. Isn't that was the natives call it?"

"Dream *Reaper*. And yes, it is a demon. I know because I've dealt with something like it before," said Elise, accidentally saying more than she wanted to. Lamez put down his coffee. She was irritated, but could tell she had his attention now. "I'm only recently coming to terms with it. I've been repressing the memory since I was six."

Lamez got out his videx and motioned for her to go on.

"Inspector, the human race isn't the only species with ghosts and paranormal activity. The Tersians have a supernatural realm just like we do. Their monsters might look alien and different, but they're sourced in the same evil."

"As a scientist, how can you believe any of this, Ms. Lawson?"

"I didn't...until now. In fact, I've spent my whole life defying the paranormal existed. I've pursued only order and truth, trying desperately to make sense of a senseless universe. A universe so unfair, and so unkind. A universe that bestows a child with a powerful, but useless and dangerous gift," said Elise, her voice shaking with emotion. "A universe that took away my sister for no reason at all."

"I'm sorry. I didn't know you had a sister," said Lamez.

"I was six when my mother got the call. My sister Amanda was twelve when her friend's hover car lost its guidance system at the worst possible time. The failsafe engaged, and the car descended, but they must have been halfway over the Atlantic ocean at the time."

"Why didn't Planetary Security pick them up?" asked Lamez.

"The car hadn't been maintained properly, and the beacon was giving a false location. They lost radio contact with them a few hours later when the car ran out of power. They never found them."

Lamez put down his videx. "That's horrible."

"I loved my big sister, and missed her dearly. Every time there was a knock at the door, I expected her to be there. My parents were numb with grief themselves and didn't offer much comfort. Worse, I kept seeing her in my dreams. She would speak to me, and tell me to come find her."

Elise dried her eyes and prepared to explain what came next. Not that it mattered; he wouldn't believe her, she barely believed it herself. But it *had* happened and it made her into the scientist she was today. It was a part of her she had to accept, and something she would need to use.

"Inspector, as I've told you, my daughter Emmie can bring things in and out of her dreams. It's why the demon is showing itself. I believe it was attracted to her like a moth to a flame. It wants to use her as a portal to cross into this world."

Lamez nodded and reviewed his notes, "And you also think the disease they are facing is because this thing is contaminating their dream world. Sick in their dreams, sick in reality too, do I have that right?"

"Yes. The demon isn't supposed to be in Tersedasia and its presence there is corrupting the place. It's like a dropping the carcass of a dead animal in a watering hole. Since all Tersians visit it when they sleep, it's a perfect way to weaken them so the demons can take over their world. It's why we can't find any pathogens. We were looking in the wrong place."

"So, about your daughter's...um, abilities, what do they have to do with you?"

"Everything! It's all my fault, all of this is my fault," Elise put her head in her hands and sobbed, hating to cry in front of him. Collecting herself, she continued quietly, "She inherited those abilities from me. I was born with them too."

"You?" he asked in surprise. "I'm sorry, but do you have proof of any of this?"

The corners of her mouth rose a little, "Oh there's been lots of proof. My mother was always finding strange things in bed with me in the morning. Strange, how I had forgotten that. I've forgotten so much."

"So you say," said Lamez. "That's something else I find hard to believe. Why did you repress all this?"

"Because of what happened, Inspector," said Elise. "You must know, I was very young, and desperate to have my sister back. I didn't think I was doing anything wrong, so one night, I brought her out of the dream with me. It didn't go so well."

"What do you mean?"

"She came back, but only in body, not in soul...at least not with *her* soul. A demon possessed her immediately, at first acting like my sister, then something else entirely; something cruel and deadly—something evil. She almost killed my parents when they restrained her."

Lamez nearly dropped his videx.

"We had to witness this perversion of my sister for three days before I was finally able to send her back. I was in a coma for a week afterwards. When I finally woke, I had no recollection of what I had done or what had happened, and I expect my parents thought it best not to remind me."

"They were probably right," said Lamez wiping his forehead. "But seriously, a demon?"

"Yes. Demons must be patient opportunists. They're everywhere waiting...wanting desperately to leave the confines of their existence and break into reality. I knew something was wrong with my sister the instant I looked into her eyes—the eyes of a monster. I saw those eyes in the creature chasing my daughter. It wants to possess her, and force her to bring it here."

"So why all the deaths? Why is this animal...er...demon, only killing kids?"

Elise thought for a moment. "Somehow, only Emmie is plugged into Tersedasia when she dreams. I don't know how yet. It's possibly the demon's influence. But because she's been there, it's knows she has an ability it needs. However, since lots of sleeping children appear in Tersedasia, and it's made mistakes trying to find her. I think it kills them when they aren't able to do what it wants."

"And you really think you'll be able to send me there to kill this thing?"

"Not me, Inspector. Emmie."

* * *

"Namu is not my boyfriend, you little twerp!" shouted Amanda. Emmie laughed as the tips of the Tersian's pointed ears turned a light shade of blue, indicating embarrassment.

"Da da's got a boyfriend! Da da's got a boyfriend!" sang Emmie, skipping out of the control room and into the main lab, where her mother was waiting.

Amanda's face reddened as she turned to her friend. "Sorry about that."

"Zis okay. Sister zis strong, she will do well," said Namu, amused. He adjusted a feather on one of his arrows before returning it to the quiver on his back. His face and chest were decorated with traditional war paint and he looked ready for anything.

Through a large, reinforced window, they watched the technicians busily setting up the experiment. The lab looked more like a hospital room than a research facility. A tech connected a set of wires to a bulky machine at the rear of two beds. Something in the control room beeped. The tech faced the window and waved for the boy to come into the lab.

"They call for me. No worry, I keep sister safe," reassured Namu.

Amanda held his hand and kissed him lightly on the cheek. His ears went bright blue as she explained, "For luck. It's an Earthie tradition."

Namu bowed and said something to her in his own language that sounded beautiful despite its oddly disjointed rhythm.

"What does that mean?" asked Amanda, surprised.

"I tell you in morning," said Namu, smiling broadly, as he turned to leave.

* * *

"But I don't wanna go to sleep!" Sitting up defiantly, Emmie fought with her mother. She didn't like the wires attached to her forehead and chest, and wasn't going down easy. Besides, the bed was stiff and scratchy, and there were too many strange people around.

"Please Emmie. I know you're scared, but Namu is in the bed next to you, and Inspector Lamez and I will be sitting right here. Once you're asleep, you can bring both of us inside with you. Make sure you bring both of us, okay?"

"Okay mama. I'll try," said Emmie. "Can Mr. Warbles come too?"

"Yes, sweetie," said Elise, handing her the bear and a glass of warm milk. She hated having to involve her daughter in this, but Emmie was the only one that could dream of Tersedasia and take them there as well. Elise had to do something or the nightmare would only get worse. Besides, the EKG and heart rate monitors would alert the techs if anything dangerous was happening and could wake her.

"The S'pecter gonna shoot the monster, Mama?" asked Emmie, yawning.

Elise met Lamez's eyes and smiled. He looked incredibly nervous for someone that didn't believe any of this was possible. He smiled back at her, then at her daughter. "I'm gonna make sure it never hurts anyone ever again, Emmie. I promise."

"Ok..." said Emmie. She snuggled under the covers and closed her eyes.

Elise watched the monitors as her daughter slept. After about an hour, she spoke to the techs in the control room over the intercom. "Mark the time on the log and start recording. She just entered REM sleep a few minutes behind Namu."

Elise marveled at the alpha wave readings. "Are you guys getting this? Her alpha waves are nearly identical to the boy's. They're having exactly the same dream."

The tech replied immediately, "Yes, but something else just happened. Emmie's readings just showed a massive transient spike near the 7.8Hz range. It's gone off the chart—"

Before Elise could reply, Lamez exploded into a tornado of wet leaves and mud. She raised her arms to protect her face as it filled the air. Knocked sideways to the floor, she watched the muck fall haphazardly around the bed.

Surprised and annoyed, she cursed under her breath for not preparing for the potential violence of the mass exchange. Still, the experiment was working. Emmie had pulled Lamez into the dream. She looked at the bed and realized Mr. Warbles had made it there again as well. *But why was she still here? And more importantly, why was Lamez's laser rifle still propped against the bed?*

* * *

"Demon is here. Don't move," said Namu as the threesome crouched behind a large outcropping of rock and moss. He slowly and quietly drew an arrow to his bow.

Lamez had no intention of moving, he was still in shock. One moment he was in the lab, and in the next he was outside, in some sort of forest, being told to be quiet by the Tersian boy. His shock didn't last long. His training took over, and took in his surroundings. Apparently, Lawson wasn't crazy—this place really existed. That meant the demon probably existed as well. He reached for his laser rifle, but it wasn't there.

"Emmie, where's my gun?" he whispered.

Emmie sat huddled on the ground, with her hands over her ears, trying to block out the incessant chittering that surrounded them. She shook her head from side to side. The poor girl looked terrified. He patted her head. "Don't worry Emmie. I'm here. It's going to be okay."

Lamez did a quick inventory. His service pistol was still strapped to his belt, which was good. In addition, the boy had chosen an excellent hiding spot for both protection and observation. He followed the boy's gaze into the clearing but could see nothing but dark shadows.

"Where is it?" he hissed to Namu, forming puffs of vapor as the temperature dropped.

"Everywhere," replied the boy. "Watch shadows."

Dark fingers rolled slowly across the clearing, as if alive, probing into crevasses and up the stalks of trees. They were getting closer and closer. Namu let loose an arrow. Lamez watched it swish into the clearing and embed itself into what, *a tree*? Something howled and the floating arrow moved through the air of its own accord, bounding towards them.

"Shoot Inspector! Shoot!" shouted Namu, letting loose more arrows which quickly joined the first.

The Inspector expertly aimed his pistol and emptied five rounds at the collection of arrows approaching them. The demon slowed, then stopped midway across the clearing, growling ominously. A hideous scream filled the air as the shadows retracted into the creature, and its powerful, muscular body flickered into view. Lamez could see the arrows and bullet holes arrayed along a scaled, tortured back, which ended in a long and powerful forked tail. It's large, bat-like wings were folded back to avoid the steam emanating from the wounds, which to Lamez's horror, seemed to be rapidly healing.

"What are you?" he asked out loud, unable to stop himself.

The demon leveled it four burning red eyes at him and with a burning chill, Lamez knew exactly what it was. It was *injustice*. It was every wife beating asshole, every molesting pervert, and every murdering bastard that through one loophole or the other, escaped justice in the courts. Well, not this time. This time, he was judge and jury; this time he was the executioner. He aimed his pistol and emptied his remaining ten rounds directly at its massive head.

A horn shattered, and one of its eyes turned into a darkened bloody socket. The demon roared in pain, defiantly showing rows of razor sharp, needle-like teeth. It lunged at them, tearing huge chunks of dirt out of the ground with its wicked claws as it launched into the air, its two huge wings spread wide open.

In a rush of steam, it sailed over the outcropping, claws extended. Before Larez could do anything to stop it, the demon grabbed Namu like a giant vulture, pulling him kicking and screaming, pumping the heated air with its wings as it rose into the air.

"Emmie! I need my laser rifle! We need more help! Where's your mother?"

Emmie was still in a ball, shaking back and forth. At first, Lamez thought she didn't hear him, but then something flashed brightly in the clearing. When his eyes readjusted, he saw the small form of Elise standing bewildered in the clearing.

Lamez yelled at her and pointed madly at the sky. The shadow of something large passed over her as she looked up. The demon, silhouetted against the larger of two moons, looked like an impossibly large bat with its prey dangling beneath it—and it was coming right at her.

In a whirlwind followed by a another bright flash, the laser rifle appeared next to Elise. Lamez was impressed at how quickly she seized the weapon, flipped off the safety and fired. A bolt of searing blue light illuminated the forest as the laser tore a huge hole in the demon's left wing, sending the creature into a spiral plummet.

It helicoptered down into the clearing, howling in rage and pain, dropping Namu in the process. The boy fell through the trees, breaking branch after branch as he plummeted to the ground into a motionless heap.

The falling monster hurtled into the clearing, cratering itself deep into the decaying forest floor with a tremendous crash. The hiss of steam emanated from inside the hole. From his vantage point, he saw the steaming gap in the demon's wing was already half the size it was only seconds earlier. Also, the wounds on its back had completely disappeared. However, the injuries on its head were bloody as ever. Only three eyes glared menacingly at him from out of the pit.

"Give me the rifle Elise! It's not dead yet, but I think I know how to kill it!" he shouted to her.

Elise ran across the clearing to the outcropping, but stumbled on a large rock and fell headlong near the pit. A taloned hand reached out and grabbed her leg. She screamed in pain as the burning claw dug into her flesh, pulling her roughly to the ground.

"Elise!" shouted Lamez, running to the pit. He only needed to cross a few hundred feet, but it might as well have been miles. Everything moved in slow motion. It wasn't supposed to go like this. He never should have let her come here. His heart sank as her legs disappeared over the lip of crater.

Elise dug her fingers into the soft mud, trying desperately to hold on. She looked up pleadingly at Lamez, but he could tell she knew he wasn't going to make it. She unslung the rifle and tossed it out in front of her. "Take it! Save my daughter!"

She slipped over the edge, kicking and screaming as the demon dragged her into the hole. He knew he would never see her again as he winced at the horrible sound of breaking bones and rendered flesh. It was over. She was gone. In a roar that froze his heart, the demon tossed her broken body out of the pit—*in two bloody pieces.*

He skidded to a halt and tearfully picked up the discarded laser rifle. Wiping his eyes, he cleared the trigger of mud and quickly ramped up the charge. Elise would be the last life this thing would take.

The demon climbed slowly out of the pit one bloody claw after the other. Seeing the Inspector, it made a horrible, hitching, clicking sound. Alien as it was, Lamez knew a laugh when he heard it, and how it had enjoyed killing her. In its three remaining eyes, he saw the exquisite pleasure it took in his pain of loss.

Well, those eyes were about to feast on something else.

Lamez picked up the laser rifle. Holding the weapon that Elise had given her life to bring, he aimed and fired at the laughing monstrosity's eyes. One by one, they exploded in balls of fire and went dark. The creature's surprised face went slack and it lost all strength, unable to hold itself upright. It slid backwards into the pit, and the chittering, whispering voices faded away.

In the silence that remained, its body shrank, shriveling into a blackened, distorted mass of flesh. Lamez blasted it again with the laser, vaporizing what was left. "Dead in the dream, dead in reality," he murmured, dropping the laser.

"S'pecter? Is it over? Where's my mama?" asked Emmie, peeking over the outcropping.

Lamez didn't want to turn around. He didn't want to face the daughter of the woman who selflessly gave her life for theirs. How could he tell that poor little girl that he wasn't able to protect her mother? Instead, he watched in silence as the sun rose before him, changing the forest dramatically, filling it with color and life. Namu's body disappeared, quietly returning to the real world.

"Send me back, so I can wake you, Emmie. We need to go home now," said the Inspector, choking back tears.

"You're crying. Are you scared? You can take Mr. Warbles if you want," said Emmie, handing him the bear.

"Thank you, sweetheart."

"Ok. S'pecter. Close your eyes."

* * *

"Wake up Emmie. It's mama. It's time to wake up."

Emmie opened her eyes and smiled sleepily at the face of her mother, and the Inspector. Behind them, Amanda was wrapping a bandage around a splint on Namu's arm.

"Did we do it, mama? Is it gone?" she asked.

"Yes, we did honey. But you did especially great," said Elise, handing Emmie her bear. "You and Mr. Warbles aren't going to have any more nightmares."

Lamez cupped Elise's shoulder warmly and smiled. "I don't even want to think about how to start the paperwork on this. I still can't believe you're alive. You really had me scared."

"I didn't exactly have time to tell you the details, did I?" She smiled into his deep brown eyes. She hadn't noticed until now how handsome he was. "When Emmie didn't bring me and the rifle into the dream, I took matters into my own hands. It had been years since I used my gift, but I knew it was still there."

"But you said you could only bring things in and out of your own dreams. So how did you dream yourself into Tersedasia? I thought only Emmie could do that."

"I took a sedative and backfed Emmie's alpha wave recording into the EKG electrodes. I used it to synchronize my brain's alpha wave pattern with hers. It was an untested theory, but it worked. I was able to dream of Tersedasia. So, instead of being pulled bodily into the dream by my daughter like you were, I simply dreamed myself there like she did."

"So, when you died—"

"I just woke up, just like any other human being. Tersians aren't so lucky." She motioned towards Namu. "When he took a beating there, he woke up in shock with a broken arm here."

"And bringing in the rifle? That was you too?"

"Yes. I hadn't done that since I was little girl. I was terrified of my power until now—I still am. It's a dangerous gift, especially in the hands of a five-year-old. It's something we will have to learn to control together."

"Do you think we'll see any more of those creatures?" asked Lamez.

"As long as Emmie and I stay out of Tersedasia, I don't think we'll have any more trouble. I pretty sure I can rig up an alpha wave generator that will keep us from going there again."

"You certainly have an unusual family," said Lamez. Then, moving a little closer and taking her hand, he said, "We're all very glad you're still with us."

"Were you really scared for me?" asked Elise, looking into those deep brown eyes.

"Very much. I didn't know how much until I lost you," said Lamez, leaning in.

"Mama's got a boyfriend!" laughed Emmie, spoiling the moment, making them back away and grin.

Lamez rubbed the back of his neck sheepishly, "Look Elise, you wanna get some breakfast or something?"

"Sure," she said, smiling at his boyish charm. "Fighting demons always works up an appetite. Then, you know what? I'm going home to get some sleep."

An Open Book

A note to the reader...

Screw you. Screw you, your family, your friends, your boss, your doctor, your plumber and your idiot mechanic. Screw your home, your job, your car, your clothes and your goddamn wide-screen TV. Screw your beliefs, your doubts, your fears, your hates and your desires. But most of all— and above all else—*screw you.* It's because of *you*, that I no longer have a family. It's because of *you* that I no longer have a home. It's because of *you* that I no longer have anything to live for.

It's all because of YOU.

Please, if there is an ounce of decently in you, *do not* read any further.

Sincerely,
Jacob Caldwell

"I think he's going to make it," murmured a disembodied voice over the "beep-beep" of a heart monitor. Jacob Caldwell blinked open his right eye; the left one didn't seem to work anymore. He saw two blurry figures standing next to his bed, speaking with each other. Both were wearing lab coats. The taller of the two took notice of his stirring. "Welcome back Mr. Caldwell," said the young doctor, surprised. "Wha... what the hell happenned?" asked Jacob dryly. He tried look around, but the left side of his head felt like a lead weight.

 "Try not to move, Jacob. You were in an accident two weeks ago, and you've had massive head trauma," said the nurse. "You need to rest." "Accident... two weeks ago?" he stammered, trying to rise. "Please Mr. Caldwell, lie still. Nurse Thompson will fill you in later," said the doctor, shining a pen light in his eye. "I'm pleased to see you are recovering so quickly. We had feared perhaps there would be extensive brain damage, even after the operation. How do you feel?"

 "Like I've been kicked in the head by a goddamn mule."

 "Actually, you were kicked in the head by a semi. Before you and your car went over the bridge, the truck's front wheel did a number on your head." "Bridge?"

"Yes... if it wasn't for the frigid water and the quick response of the rescue unit, you would have died of your injuries." "I... I don't remember..." his voice trailed off as a wave of exhaustion gripped him. He couldn't stay conscious much longer. "Nurse, please notify Mr. Caldwell's wife and children that he's back with us," the doctor said, handing her back Caldwell's chart. "I'll phone the Cybernetics Director personally with the news."

* * *

"I'm telling you... I'm hearing things... I dunno... *voices*," said Caldwell. "At first, I thought they were just my thoughts, but they aren't in *my* voice. Sometimes it's the voice of a man, sometimes it's a woman. Also, they're getting louder and harder to ignore. And what they are saying is weird; it's sorta like a narrative echo of whatever I'm doing." "And are these voices speaking to you now?" asked the cybernetics technician, checking the readings on her display. A pulsing fiber-link cable ran from her monitoring computer to a plug in the left side of Caldwell's head. "Yes, but right now it's just barely audible over the background noise." "Background noise?"

"I told you about that last month. Ever since you people replaced the left side of my head with this... this *infernal machine*... I've been hearing a low crackle and hiss." At that moment, the Cybernetics Director stepped through the open door of the therapy room. He wasn't smiling. "Mr. Caldwell, the infernal machine you refer to cost over two million dollars, has over a billion quantum-sized components and represents twenty years of work," he chastised. "Need I remind you that it's the only reason you are alive today?" "Shit Doc... it's not that I'm not appreciative, but no one is taking me seriously damnit!" he said angrily. "The voices again?"

"Yeah... like just now. When you came in, they got a little louder. It sounded like I was being read to... like I was listening to an audio book." "Really? What did it say?" "Well, it was talking about you. It said, 'At that moment, the Cybernetics Director stepped through the open door...' " Suddenly, Caldwell gripped the sides of his head, "Argghh" The Director rushed to his side in alarm. "What's wrong?" Caldwell cursed under his breath, "I'm... I'm okay... I just had one bitch of a headache." The technician looked up from her display. "His brain activity just now was spiking off the chart." "In which area?" asked the Director. "Mostly in the temporal lobe—which is probably why he's hearing things—but also in the prefrontal cortex as well, which is really odd." "Hmmm... Jacob, how do you feel? Do you feel like yourself?" asked the Director. "Doc... I haven't felt like myself since the accident. I can't remember shit, and my wife thinks I'm going crazy." "Well, the impact destroyed a good bit of your memory. However, the nanobots are still rebuilding as much of it as possible. You should come back to yourself in time. For now, I'll have Doctor Lambert increase your pain medication." "Can you do anything about these freaky voices?" "Right now, we're just trying to keep you stabilized. Maybe in another week or so we'll have a good enough baseline to make refinements. For now, you'll have to live with it and the background noise. Try to ignore it the best you can." "Director, he's starting to spike again." He looked towards the monitor, trying to hide his concern. Earlier experiments with the quantum brain had showed similar spikes in the animal test subjects. A few days later, they became lethargic and unresponsive. Eventually, they died. "What? Am I going to die?" panicked Caldwell. "Uh... what do you mean?" asked the Director, caught off guard. "Your earlier tests on animals... they became lethargic and unresponsive... then they died, didn't they?" "Yes... but how did you know that?" "It was just read to me."

* * *

"Jacob, you're scaring me. I think it would be best if I took the kids to mother's until this passes." Helen had been unsure of her husband ever since the operation. He hadn't come back the same man, and now this thing with hearing voices… it wasn't natural. She wished he could just turn his new quantum brain off."

"Damnit Helen. You know I can't just turn it off," he shouted at her angrily. Since leaving the Cybernetics lab, he had enjoyed a few voice-free days, but now it was back, loud and clear.

"But I didn't say that outloud…" she started.

"You didn't have to. It was *read* to me—just like everything else," said Jacob. "I've got a goddamn screenplay running in my head."

There was a knock at the front door. The Cybernetics Director waited outside, fumbling with his umbrella. Suddenly, the wind caught it and sent it sailing across the yard. He watched it go despondently. *If one more thing goes wrong tonight I'm going to blow my brains out,* he thought.

"Helen, just get that will you?" Jacob demanded.

His wife went to the door and admitted their guest. Jacob didn't even turn around, he just reclined on the sofa and stared at the wall in front of him.

"Hello Director," said Jacob. "Please, don't blow out your brains on my account. I'll get you another umbrella before you leave."

"So it's still happening, then?" asked the Director as he handed Helen his coat.

She nodded and put it on the wall hook. Her eyes filled with tears and she ran upstairs. This was all too much for a small-town wife with two young kids to handle. She would pack their suitcases and be out of the house before her husband realized they were gone.

"Fine! Get the hell out of here. Who needs you?" shouted Jacob after her.

"Jacob. We have a problem," said the Director.

"I'll say we do. My wife thinks I'm a freak, and my kids won't speak to me."

"No, it's more serious than that. I need you to come with me to the lab, *tonight.*"

"Screw you Doc. I've got bigger fish to fry than helping out with more tests. My traitorous wife is leaving me! Where do you get off, dragging me out of my own house in the middle of the night?"

Just then, a thunderclap sounded outside. It was really coming down hard.

The Director stared at him with a desperate expression. "I'm sorry for you Jacob. Truly I am… please, don't think I'm minimizing your problems. But you must understand, this thing concerns more than just you and your family."

 "Wait a minute… you're serious? What's going on?"

"We have a theory about the voices, but I need you to test them. Then we'll know for sure."

"I thought it wasn't about me?"

"It's not. It's about the nature of the voices. I fear your episodes are just the tip of a much, much larger iceberg. Please, I'm begging you, come back with me to the lab."

The Director was trying hard to reason with the man, but if he continued to resist, he'd use his backup plan. Distasteful as it was, he would use the syringe of sedative if Caldwell forced the issue.

"Empty your pockets, Doc." said Jacob, deadpan.

"What? Why?" stammered the Director.

"I want that syringe."

The Director flushed in surprise, but handed the

needle to Caldwell. "It's really true then, isn't it? You're being—how did you describe it—*narrated* to?"

"Yep. Someone is reading about us right now. You know that little voice inside your head you hear when you read a book, Doc? Well, I can hear *theirs*. I know this because it's not always the same voice. I think that sometimes other people do the reading."

The Director thought for a moment. "Actually, that fits with my hypothesis. I can explain more in the car. Are you coming or not?"

"Shit doc, if it's important enough for you to drug and kidnap me, I guess maybe I should."

* * *

"So, you're saying my new brain can see an alternate reality?"

"More specifically, it exists in our world and theirs at the same time," said the Director. "This is because of the quantum nature of your artificial brain. It's all been quite surprising."

"Um Doc... you told me to tell you when the voice came back. Well, it's back. It's the same one from when you picked me up. It's reading about us again," said Jacob.

A boom sounded outside the lab and the lights flickered. The storm beat heavily against the windows as lightning flashed nearby. *What kind of weather was this?* Jacob wondered.

The Director rechecked Caldwell's fiber-link connection, went to the terminal and pressed a button. A static-filled window opened on the display. "Mary, try to filter out the random action potentials would you?"

"Yes Doctor." The technician made a few adjustments and an image of a face began to solidify.

"Jacob Caldwell, I'd like you to meet your *reader*."

Jacob stared at the screen and laughed.

"What's so funny?" asked the Director.

"Holy shit! Just look at that bemused expression! Is that really the face behind the voice I'm hearing?"

"Well, it's only a still image, granted. But it's the best we can do. It's more or less the image they have of themselves at this point in time. When another reader picks up the book, the face will change the same way the voice does."

"What exactly do you mean by *book?*"

"Mary, switch to the occipital lobe feed. Show him what the reader sees."

Another window opened, but this time, instead of a face, blurry text appeared in neat rows. Jacob read a few lines at the top. They mirrored everything he had heard in his head recently.

"Is this what they are reading? There's actually a real book or something? How is that possible? Who wrote it?"

"We don't know. Somehow a writer in their world saw into ours and wrote all this down."

"What do you mean *wrote?* How could things be written down that haven't happened yet? I saw lots more text past the point I was hearing, but it gave me a headache to try and read it."

The wind outside began to howl. The Director looked nervously at the creaking windows as they flexed and shuddered.

"I don't know how he did it, but quantum theory treats time as simply another dimension, just as adjustable as the other three. Unfortunately, that brings us to the issue at hand. I fear our world may be in danger of a temporal collapse."

"What do you mean?"

"Have you been feeling a sensation of deja vu since the accident?"

"You mean, like all this has happened before? Yeah... I think so. I think that's what has kept me from becoming a raving lunatic. It's like I'm *used* to it."

"Well, I believe that it stems from the fact that this book is being read over and over, by countless people. Each time someone reads it, our world goes through another temporal loop. Eventually, we will wear out this little part of space-time and cause a rupture that will unravel everything."

"So, you're telling me that because a bunch of vicarious little shits want to be entertained, our world will come to an end?"

"Yes."

"How do we stop it?"

"I think it's already too late."

Another crash of thunder and the power went completely out. The windows exploded at nearly the same moment. Mary screamed as they dived for cover behind a work bench.

"This isn't a regular storm, is it?" asked Jacob,

unplugging the fiber-link from his head.

"No, I think it's starting," said the Director.

"I've got to try something." said Jacob, clearing his voice.

"Look moron. Yes, I'm talking to you *dear reader.* This is not a joke. You are screwing with real people here. Millions of people will die because of you and people like you."

"Jacob… I don't think that will…" started the Director.

"Look, if time is as flexible as you say, we might have a chance. Maybe the asshole that wrote this story will hear what I'm about to say. If he doesn't take it seriously, at least maybe he will put some sort of warning at the front of the book or something."

"Yes, but…"

"Screw it! I'm going to try…"

Miasma

"You're certain it's not an asteroid?" asked President Falkirk, turning away from the Situation Room's holoscreen. He couldn't believe the presentation he just witnessed.

"Yes sir... it's definitely moving with intelligence," said Dr. Robert Aimsley, the President's disheveled Chief Scientific Advisor. He often briefed the President—mostly on the environmental crisis—but this was another matter entirely. "It's making course corrections as it travels through the solar system. The latest footage from the remote observatory on Phoebos shows it using Jupiter's gravity to slow its speed."

"How long before the object will become visible to ground-based telescopes?" asked Lieutenant General Rhodes, the National Security Advisor.

The scientist fidgeted in his chair. "Well sir, it's *already* visible. This morning, I fielded a call from what's left of the Keck Observatory in Hawaii— as you know, the island was under attack again last week."

"We think the Asian Alliance had something to do with that," started Admiral Hayes, the Secretary of Defense.

"Military affairs aside Admiral, you should know, it's only a matter of time before the object shows up prominently in the sky," said Aimsley.

The President scowled. "Dr. Aimsley, are you telling me that soon, the general public will know about this *visitor*, and there's nothing we can do about it? Why didn't you inform us earlier?"

"Sir... you don't understand how fast it's moving. We predict its arrival in less than three days. It only showed up yesterday in a routine asteroid scan."

Everyone in the cramped room started talking at once. Aimsley leaned back and rubbed his eyes, letting the President's staff come to terms with the startling information. He was exhausted from the lack of sleep.

Actually, Aimsley had known about the strange object a full day earlier, at his Radiometric's lab in California using the Hat Creek Radio Telescope Array. At the time, he assumed it was just another large asteroid among the thousands in the vast Kuiper belt surrounding the solar system. However, when the secret government telescope on Phoebos showed it banking into the ecliptic, he knew it was something else—*or more likely, someone else*—and it was making a bee-line for Earth. Aimsley and his team had been tracking the object non-stop ever since.

"Is there any chance of communicating with it?" asked the President.

"We're already sending broadband radio and laser messages from our probes around Saturn and Jupiter, but haven't received any response. We hope that as the object slows, we'll have better luck."

Hayes grunted. "I've got a few nukes that communicate real well, Mr. President. I suggest we send it a nice, warm greeting. From what I've seen, that thing looks like an incoming missile."

The President ignored the comment. Unlike his predecessors, he had no intention of shooting first, and asking questions later. That's what had made things so bad in the first place. Incessant global warming—exacerbated by heavy population growth—set an apocalyptic backdrop for massive nuclear warfare as countries battled for resources. By the turn of the twenty-second century, much of the Earth's landmass was barren, and radioactive fallout was accelerating the decline of a vanishing ecology.

"Half of the world is dead or dying, gentlemen. We have been pissing in our bath water for far too long. We've known for years that there's nothing we can do to reverse the damage. If this thing is from another world, maybe it can help."

Aimsley suppressed a smile. He liked Falkirk's optimism—it was one of the reasons he supported him—but it was somewhat naïve. Any race advanced enough to travel at such speeds, obviously had the upper hand technologically. What could we possibly offer them in exchange?

Hayes refused to back down. "No offense Mr. President, but that's a load of horse pucky. I say we destroy this invader—or whatever it is—with an ICBM. We can't afford to wait until we know its intentions."

"I appreciate your concerns Admiral Hayes, but I must disagree… and I'm sorry, did you actually just say *horse pucky?*" winced the President.

"This is no joking matter. That thing is a very real threat, and it needs to be taken out!" Hayes pounded his fist on the table to drive the point home, rattling the collection of medals on his lapel.

"I must agree with the Admiral," said Rhodes. "If we can't communicate with it, we should probably assume the worst."

"Yes, but even if we were to launch a warhead into space, the object would be in our backyard by the time the missile impacted. The debris from the explosion of something that large could fall to Earth," said Aimsley.

"Exactly how large is it?" asked Hayes.

"We estimate its size to be about one-fourth the size of the moon, but we can't discern its shape. Recent images taken by a probe around Ganymede show the object's breaking orbit simply as streaks of light."

Aimsley brought up the blurry photos from the Jovian system on the holoscreen. His staff had sent the eerie images to him during his aerolift to Washington.

"It looks like a shooting star," said the President.

"That's because it's moving so fast. It's making hundreds of increasingly wide orbits around the gas giant as it slows."

"Well gentlemen, I've seen enough. I have to prepare for a press conference," said the President, standing up. "I intend to address the Union this evening with full disclosure on the object."

Both Hayes and Rhodes protested vehemently. The President quieted them with a gesture. "Please gentlemen. If we had more time, I would obviously entertain other options. This thing is going to make itself known in a few days whether we want it to or not. I think the public would prefer to hear about it from the people they elected to be on top of such things."

Leaving the two grumbling advisors to follow in his wake, the President exited the room.

Aimsley gathered his materials quickly; he had to catch a flight to yet another meeting on his agenda. He sighed, urgently wanting to get back to his lab. He turned off the holoscreen. As the display evaporated, the streaking object faded away first, followed slowly by the rest of the image. He wished the real thing would just *disappear.* This wasn't at all what he thought a "First Contact" experience would feel like. Instead of a joyful sense of awe or wonder, he only felt a cold dread—a primal fear of the unknown. This thing was coming, and it was something no one could control. He could only hope the President's unbridled optimism would bear fruit.

* * *

Glad to be home after three days of meetings and grueling travel, Aimsley had exciting news to share with his team. Taking off his re-breather, he impatiently sealed the outer door to the Cal Tech Science Complex. The weather forecast had been right on the money for a change. The air outside was so thick with humidity and contaminants that he nearly had to swim from the aerolift parking bay.

Brushing the moisture off his tweed jacket, he quickly turned towards the lobby. *Everything was moving so fast,* he mused. It had been less than a week since the Visitor dropped into the solar system. The Visitor was what the world now called the strange object currently orbiting the moon. He smiled—soon it would have a visitor of its own.

"Good morning Dr..." started the receptionist, as Aimsley rushed past. He managed a weak wave in her direction as he turned the hallway to the Radiometrics Lab. She shrugged and turned back to the news program on her holoscreen.

"Tachyons... actual Tachyons!" Aimsley muttered excitedly to himself. He pressed his palm into the DNA scanner. It beeped, and the heavy door opened with a hiss. A young research assistant looked up from her terminal as he stepped inside the chilly lab. Unfortunately, the cold was unavoidable. Without the air conditioning, the racks of electronics in the room would quickly burn themselves out.

"Good morning, everyone. I assume you are monitoring the Aurora mission?" he asked.

Two of the three people in the room nodded enthusiastically from behind their holoscreens; the third was asleep at his terminal. Crumpled paper coffee cups filled the wastebaskets.

Someone had put up a hand written note that read, "ABANDON SLEEP, ALL YE WHO ENTER"

"Somebody wake up Professor Hawkins. I don't think he'll want to miss this," said Aimsley.

Gayle, the dozing man's bookish assistant, gave Hawkins a gentle poke in the side. His stubbled chin jerked out of a pool of spittle. After a brief moment of confusion, he straightened his hair and glasses, and glared at Gayle, who shrank away.

"Tachyons," said Aimsley simply.

"Excuse me?" asked Hawkins, yawning.

"Tachyons, my good sir. I speak of those little quantum particles of impossibility that violate causality in special relativity..."

"What about them Robert? Obviously, you're just *busting* to say something." The communications professor was obviously in a bad mood. He glowered at his clean-shaven colleague. "Look at you... what did you get in the aerolift? ...a good two hours of sleep? Must be nice..."

"Four actually... weather conditions delayed my arrival, and we had to make a few orbits," smiled Aimsley. "But look, it's not my fault they convened in Washington, then sent me all over the blasted Union. The Chief Science Advisor goes where he's told."

"So, what did this grand meeting of the minds produce?" asked Hawkins, picking something out of his teeth.

"Tachyons!" said Aimsley once again. "As unbelievable as it seems, the CIA's facility in Alaska has discovered that the Visitor is emitting Tachyons!"

The two lab assistants looked up from their displays and stared at him; even Hawkins seemed surprised by the statement.

"But Tachyons aren't detectable..." said Eoin, the research assistant Aimsley hired last week. Gayle constantly derided him as the new guy, jealous of the way he could interpret interferometry patterns faster than anyone in the room.

"My good man, I have more resources at my disposal than our little group of brilliant misfits," smiled Aimsley. "The CIA's Theoretical Research Division has been studying Tachyons for years and has found a way to detect the undetectable."

"What Theoretical Research Division? Why haven't I heard about this until now?" exclaimed Hawkins. "A breakthrough in Tachyon research would open up possibilities in communications, propulsion... hell, even time travel!"

"We might be able to do something about the conditions outside," said Gayle. "Dr. Aimsley, the world should know about this. Who are these people?"

"Well, quite honestly, I didn't know about them either, until Lieutenant General Rhodes put them on my agenda. They're part of the CIA's Special Activities Division. As to their research, until now, it was just that—*theoretical.* For some time now, they've had a working Tachyon Detection Grid, but the level of local space-time disturbances remained too low to test it—that is, until the Visitor arrived."

"This is fantastic!" said Hawkins, now fully awake. "Do they know what the Visitor is using the Tachyons for? Propulsion... communication... telemetry—*what?*"

"Yes, likely it's all three. It's too hard to tell from Earth, which is why they included the Tachyon Dectection Grid in the Aurora's science package. How is the mission proceeding?" asked Aimsley, turning to the two assistants.

"Well, they launched from the New Mexico Space Port this morning, and she should be on her way to the Visitor by now," said Eoin.

"What do you mean, *should be?*" asked Aimsley, concerned.

"Shortly after entering space and switching to Ion propulsion, the ship lost all communications. They seem to be experiencing the same radio interference that caused the temporary blackout with the New Horizon moon base. Ever since the Visitor took up residence around the moon, we've had wild fluctuations in the electromagnetic spectrum. Even ground-based communications have been disturbed."

"It's causing spectacular upper atmosphere visual effects everywhere on Earth. It's like what you'd see during a really bad solar storm," said Gayle.

"Except that there are also two moons in the sky," smirked Hawkins. "Didn't they expect to have radio interference with the Aurora?"

"Of course they did. If you had stayed awake last night, you'd know that the ship is equipped with an optical laser communicator, but they won't be able to use it until it's oriented properly," said Eoin tersely.

"How long until the two astronauts reach the Visitor?" asked Aimsley.

"About twenty minutes. If all goes well, we should hear from them shortly after they land."

* * *

"It looks like a great, dirty peanut! Are they sure this isn't just a bloody asteroid?" asked a static-filled voice in Captain Forester's helmet.

"Sure looks like one to me, Beans," said Forester as he doubled checked the landing sequence and punched in a few commands. As veteran asteroid miners, both Captain Forester and his copilot Beansby had seen lots of big rocks just like the one fast approaching in the view screen.

The Aurora slowly rotated into a nose-up position and began a rapid descent to the grey, uneven surface of the Visitor. The elegant, silver ship landed lightly on its three tail runners in billowing clouds of ancient dust and steaming water vapor. As the engines disengaged and cooled, a fine mist slowly drifted away, coiling and looping into space, unaffected by the low gravity.

An elevator platform descended from beneath the towering, cigar-shaped vessel. Two men in space suits stepped off, towing a large equipment crate.

"Crikey, it's cold out here!" said Beans.

"Yeah, this side of the snowball isn't directly facing the sun. Our suits are having a hard time keeping us warm. Also, the radiation level is very high. We won't be able to stay very long. Let's just get the job done and get the hell out of here," said Forester.

"Too right mate," said Beans, opening the crate. "This place puts the willies up me."

Looking for a flat place to setup the equipment, Forester slowly scanned the terrain. Like most of the asteroids he visited, the soil was rocky and loose, barely held together by the ice and frost. As he turned, he could feel the ground beneath him shift under his weight—as if he were walking on corn flakes. The Visitor felt more and more like just another asteroid.

"Beans, you've been on the mining run to Tuttle. Are you thinking what I'm thinking?"

"What? That this is just a rogue asteroid, and we're freezing our arses off for no good reason? Then yeah, I'm thinkin' it. When I get back, some blooming git in Washington is gonna get a right good..." his voice trailed off. "Oi... what's that over there?"

Both men stared at the desolate horizon opposite the ship. A bright blue point of light flashed briefly then disappeared.

A few seconds later, it flashed again—only a little more intensely.

"That's odd... it looks like some sort of beacon," proposed Forester. "We can go exploring later. For now, let's get the science package and the laser operational... we need to check in with mission control."

The two men unpacked two basketball-sized pieces of equipment. Setting the science package aside, they focused on the laser communications device first. Planting its tripod firmly in the asteroid's surface, Beans switched it on, calibrated the optics, and gave the thumbs up.

Forester spoke into his helmet. "Capcom... This is Captain Forester of the Aurora. Do you read me?"

A few seconds later, through a burst of static, came a response. "Glad to hear from you Captain. What's your status?"

"The mission is proceeding according to schedule. The Visitor looks exactly as imagery from New Horizon suggested. It appears to be simply a large, rogue asteroid. However, we saw a strange light about five clicks spinward of our direction. Should we check it out?"

"Negative. Activate the science package and return to the ship. During the Aurora's orbital scan, you can investigate the area using the ship's sensors."

"Copy Capcom... Forester out."

He bent over and spent five minutes configuring the complex device. After attaching a fiber optic link to the laser communicator, he turned around to face his oddly quiet companion.

"Okay Beans, that should do it. Capcom now wants us to... Beans? Beans! What's wrong?"

Forester stared at his friend. Beans' expressionless face was glowing strangely, and his eyes—*God, what had happened to his eyes?* They were now orbs of intense blue light... exactly like the pulsing blue light over the horizon.

* * *

"We have the laser communicator feed from the Visitor, Dr. Aimsley!" exclaimed Eoin, watching the streams of data pouring into his holoscreen.

"Wonderful, wonderful!" said Aimsley, nudging the others aside. "I can't believe we're getting this. The Tachyon Detection Grid in the science package is working beautifully."

"I'll start separating the data streams now," said Eoin. "It'll take a while for the computer to work out the best algorithm."

"That's fine Eoin. You've done a great job. Why don't you and Gayle catch up on a little sleep? Professor Hawkins and I can do the housekeeping on the data stream until the computer is ready. I'll need both of you to be well rested for what comes next."

The two assistants were far too excited for sleep, but at his insistence, they cleared off the two sofas in Hawkins' office. Not surprisingly, they were fast asleep before Aimsely returned to the lab.

"Well, this is certainly interesting," said Hawkins, as Aimsley took the seat next to him.

"What is?"

"From the preliminary data, it looks like our rocky friend is sending a Tachyon stream back the way it came."

"It's not just a residual echo from its journey through the solar system?"

"Robert, we know so little about Tachyons that I don't think anyone—not even those eggheads in the Theoretical Research Division—could answer that with any certainty. But I can tell it's a dynamic, changing signal, so I don't think it's a propulsion echo."

"I expect we'll know more in the morning when the computer finishes its analysis. In the meantime, keep an eye on the signal to noise ratio. We need to make the data as clean as possible so that the computer has more to work with," said Aimsley. "I'll take the next shift in an hour or so."

"What are you going to be doing in the meantime?"

"I'm going to make sure the President includes me via holocast when they debrief the astronauts tomorrow. Then I'm going to find some of that awful sludge you people call coffee."

* * *

"Mr. President, I'm telling you. That thing spoke to me... and it spoke of *love*," said Beans, smiling beatifically.

"I'm sorry Mr. Beansby, but I find this all a little hard to believe. Captain, can you back up his story?" asked the President, turning to Forester.

"All I can say sir, is that while we were up there, Beans here was in some sort of trance for about ten minutes. His face and eyes weren't normal. I've seen all kinds of space madness in my twenty years, but I ain't never seen anything like that. I've known Beans for more than half that time, and I can tell you, he isn't the same man he used to be. That thing did something to him up there."

Beans smiled at his friend before turning to the President. "They love us, Mr. President. That's what it told me. Up there, I've never felt so... well... so bloomin' appreciated. Like it cared about every bleedin' thing I ever did—even the things I ain't so proud of. It was *assessing* me."

"He's turned into a goddamn space hippie," muttered Admiral Hayes.

"I noticed you said *they*... does that mean there's more of these things? Who are they?" asked the National Security Advisor.

Beans' had a hard time answering the question. "Well, it's like this, General Rhodes... it didn't use words, it just gave me impressions about things, using my own memories. It was as if we were playing a bizarre game of emotional charades. I just *felt* as if it was communicating on the behalf of others."

"So, there's a chance you might have misunderstood something?" asked President Falkirk.

"Yeah, I guess so… but I got two or three things right loud and clear. The Visitor is a probe or something, and its primary job is to *assess.* It's piloted by a living entity who is incredibly ancient and nearly immortal. They live for millions of years. They are infinitely patient and plan things along staggering time frames. That leads me to something else… apparently, we've got a history with these things. They know us intimately, as a father knows a son…"

"These things are the fathers of mankind? Oh, that'll go over great with the Christians…" said Hayes.

"Well, I don't know if I'd go that far. It just showed me an old memory. It brought back the time I smashed up my dad's Bentley when I was twelve. I got a right whoppin' for that, but I deserved it. Sure, he was disappointed in me for stealin' the car, but I knew he still loved me. It was kinda like that."

"Horse puckey," grumbled Hayes. "I still say we should nuke it."

The President ignored the Admiral. The man was a brilliant tactician, but he always wanted to *nuke* something. Rolling his eyes, he turned to the flickering image of his Chief Science Advisor in the holoscreen. "Dr. Aimsley, have your people made any progress communicating with the Visitor?" asked the President.

"Yes sir... my team is making excellent progress. For a technology so incredibly alien, they have been working miracles all morning. From what we can see, the Visitor appears to be scanning the entire planet. It's measuring temperature, weather, air and water pollution, radiation and the general health of the biosphere—we don't exactly know why. We should have a better understanding soon."

"Well then, keep me briefed on your progress. This thing seems to be friendly for the moment, so we'll wait a little longer before taking any drastic action," said the President, frowning at Admiral Hayes. He extended his hand to Forester. "Captain, you and your colleague have done an excellent job. Let us know if Mr. Beansby has any further revelations concerning the Visitor."

"Thank you sir, I will. Just keep in mind, we're both pretty tired. We were rushed over here shortly after re-entry. Beans' wife hasn't even been told about the incident yet. I don't know what she'll make of the man I've brought back."

* * *

"You were right! It's using a visual method of communication!" said Gayle, giving Eoin a bear hug. The boy blushed as she squeezed the life out of him.

The three of them had been working on the Visitor's Tachyon stream for hours, but could not discern a pattern. Hawkins had been certain it was a transmission, but it didn't match any known patterns of analog or digital exchange. However, after being told that one of the astronauts had communicated visually with the entity, Eoin had the idea to interpret the data using a visual three-dimensional representation.

Now, flickering orange and gold specks danced and blurred over a pulsing, cobalt-blue sphere of energy in his holoscreen. The image was incredibly captivating. The seemingly random pattern of colors brought up memories of things he hadn't thought of for years—*unpleasant ones.* Less than a minute later, Gayle was sobbing next to him.

Hawkins wheeled his chair over to where the two assistants sat enraptured by the screen. "You two have something? Hey… Gayle, what's wrong?"

Cupping her shoulder, he turned her around to face him. Her tear-stained face was glowing softly. "Oh my God, Gayle... *your eyes!*"

Turning to Eoin, he saw that the boy's eyes glowed with the same intense blue light. He followed his gaze to the strange, flashing image on the holoscreen. He quickly switched it off, but the boy continued to stare in horror at the empty air in front of him. Slowly, he crumpled to the floor.

Gayle went limp next, but Hawkins caught her and shook her vigorously. "Gayle! Snap out of it! Gayle! It's me... Professor Hawkins!"

After a few seconds, the light in her eyes faded, replaced first by a flash of confusion, then by abject terror. She screamed, and tried to pull away from him. Her fists beat against his chest until she finally collapsed, sobbing in his arms.

Eoin had curled up into a fetal position. His skin went pale and clammy. He was shivering and completely unresponsive to any attempts to revive him.

"It was... protecting itself. I think..." said Gayle in a quiet, shaking voice. "I think it knew somehow that we were there. Eoin must have seen much more, before it... it..."

Hawkins looked her in the eye and spoke softly. "Gayle… I need you to get out of here. Go find Dr. Aimsley and tell him to call for an ambulance. The boy is in shock. I'll do what I can for him until you get back."

"But Professor Hawkins… you don't understand… the Visitor, it's not what we think…" started Gayle.

"We can talk later. For now, go get Dr. Aimsley," said Hawkins firmly. "He should be in the conference room down the hall."

* * *

As a medic took Eoin's pulse, Gayle explained a little of what she had seen to Aimsley and Hawkins. Aimsley's eyes grew wide with alarm. He opened a secure line to the White House. "I don't care if the President is in a meeting with Jesus Christ, get him on the line *immediately!*"

Eoin pushed the oxygen mask away. "I'm fine now… really."

"Well, your pulse is still pretty high. I'd really prefer you go to a hospital," said the medic.

"We don't have time for that… I need to speak with the President."

"Tell me what happened, son. I've got him on the line," said Aimsley.

"We need to destroy the Visitor. It's not what we thought... *nothing is—anymore.*"

"Gayle said it's going to wipe us out? Is that true? I thought it told Beansby that we were its children?" asked Aimsley.

"No, no, no... Beansby got it all wrong. It's not a father-son love, it's more like the appreciation a farmer has for the worms he puts in his garden. Like the worms, we were made to prepare the Earth—*for them.*"

"What? As a race, we've only managed to kill most of the life on the planet, completely ruin the ecology and nearly bomb ourselves to death. How is that beneficial to anyone?" asked Gayle.

"It's beneficial to *them*. They thrive on hot, arid environments and breathe a mixture of carbon dioxide, methane, and nitrous oxide. They even favor high levels of background radiation. To them, the damnable place we call Earth is a paradise."

"Are you saying they *made* us?" asked Hawkins.

"Not exactly... it's more like they corrupted us. Because they live so long, they are in a constant search for new worlds to support their population growth. Not many planets have the conditions they need to survive, so they have to *terraform* them. They do this the most efficient way possible—by using the indigenous species. They spread a biological agent they call the *Miasma,* which alters the DNA of humanoid life-forms. It was introduced into our atmosphere early in our development. Since then, everything we've ever done has been by their design."

"You learned all this just from the communication stream?" asked Hawkins, incredulously.

"The Visitor's race can somehow generate and use Tachyons inherently. Besides altering asteroids for basic shelter, they don't use much technology. When we tapped into the communication stream, we were really tapping into its *mind.* I saw too much, and it almost killed me."

"Surely, this Miasma of theirs can be fought," said Gayle. "What about all the people that want to clean up the environment, or stop all the fighting?"

"When we detour too far from our pre-programmed nature, they send a probe like the Visitor to set things back on track. They've been here many times, reseeding the skies," said Eoin.

"They probably use meteors for distribution," proposed Aimsley. "As they fall to Earth and disintegrate, the biological agent is released—we would only see shooting stars."

"Yes, but the Visitor is the *last* probe. We must destroy before it can report its final assessment to the others. When they come, they will claim this planet as their own. We've done our job well, but like the farmer, they won't think twice about crushing us if we get in their way."

"Admiral Hayes has scrambled an ICBM from the New Horizon moon base. We should have a visual confirmation of the impact within a few minutes," said Aimsley. All four of them went to the window where the moon and its new, smaller companion hung forlornly in the smog-filled sky. Suddenly, the smaller one winked out in a bright flash.

"Well, that should do it," said Aimsley.

"I wouldn't be so sure, Robert... I think you should see this," said Hawkins, monitoring a feed from the Radio Telescope. "There's more activity in the Kuiper belt. Another large asteroid just dropped out of orbit and is heading this way."

"No problem, we can just blow it out of the sky as well," said Aimsley.

"Wait! Oh my God... there's even more now!" said Hawkins, his face turning pale.

"What? How many more?" asked Aimsley.

"All of them."

Deus ex Machina

I used to be a total klutz. My wife used to say that I was too preoccupied with whatever the project du jour was to pay attention to the little things in life. Lost in my work, things like watches, sat-coms, sunglasses, fine china, and even plate glass windows soon found themselves reduced to shattered waste in my wake. I left a trail of tears and destruction wherever I went.

So, whenever I bought a sat-com, I'd get a very durable case. Whenever I bought sunglasses, I'd make sure they had flexible frames. Whenever I bought watches...well, actually by then I'd given up completely on watches. I loved the nostalgic feel of a watch, but no one could make a crystal display I couldn't crack in less than a month, so I stopped wearing them.

This was all, of course, before I *died.* My horrific and violent demise changed many aspects of my life—no longer being distracted and clumsy was one.

I suppose that because things I valued were constantly breaking around me, it contributed to my inclination towards over-engineering. It's probably why I went overboard and made *Emma* so utterly indestructible.

I wanted to protect my work, not from my ineptitude, but from the place she was going.

From the start, Emma would be abused, of that there was no question. She would be misunderstood, treated like the others, another dumb machine doing a mindless job for the Foundry. No one would care to know the delicate intricacies underneath that impenetrable lonsdaleite shell. No one would take the time to discover what she was truly capable of.

Her new occupation would subject her to the same high temperatures, the same abrasive chemicals, and the same brutal vibrations as her co-workers. They would lump her in with the rest, expect her to fail in three years, and then replace her with the newest model. But she didn't, did she?

EMA-316 survived everything we threw at her, including me.

* * *

"Dis one's pretty, ain't she?" regarded Zeb, opening the crate that the landing bay crane had just lowered from the ship. The bay's powerful floodlights reflected brilliantly off the crate's contents and Zeb had to shield his eyes. "Hey boss, why she all sparkly and stuff?"

The foreman looked down at the scene. "Dunno. Must be the way they makin' em now. Is she the one replacin' MOE-453?" he asked, scratching his large bald head.

Zeb scanned through his duty roster until he found the entry. "Yep. She goin' to da Foundry alright. Her service code EMA-316. She's 'posed to be one of dem hotbots."

"Okay, Zeb, you know the drill. Walk her over to the shuttle and plug her in. She'll get her work orders enroute."

"You sure boss? She don't look like no hotbot."

The foreman rubbed his eyes, this was going to be a long day. Martian days were pretty much the same length as Earth's, but working with *Remies* like Zeb made them feel much longer. He leaned forward in the crane's air-conditioned cab and rapped on the window.

"You some kinda robot scientist or something, Zeb? I didn't know you reconstituted Martians were so overqualified. Maybe you want yourself another job or something?"

"Shiz, boss. I was just sayin'…"

"Move it to the truck, Zeb. Go on, get on with it. We've got a busy day."

Zeb walked EMA-316 to the shuttle and sat her down. "Just seems like a waste, is all..." he murmured to himself as he plugged her into the seat. As he leaned over to secure her restraints he whispered, "You sure are pretty."

As he backed out of the shuttle and turned towards the loading dock, he could have sworn he saw a smile on those sparkling ruby lips.

* * *

"Robert, there's someone from the Martian Foundry Authority that wants to speak with you," lilted the sultry voice of my autonomous secretary, JESS-232, over the intercom.

I designed Jess to look and sound like a real version of Jessica Rabbit, an animated character from one of those vintage films I'm so fond of. When people ask me about her appearance, I say I made her as a homage to a bygone era, but really, it was just to piss off my wife, Cynthia.

Up to my elbows in wire and hardware, I looked up from the workbench. "Now Jess? I'm right in the middle of a delicate operation."

"I know, but it's the president. It seems pretty important. But if you need more time, I can..."

"No, no...I'll take the call. Just put it through..."

"He's not on the sat-com; he's here in the reception room."

I blinked behind the cracked lenses of my magnification goggles, stunned stiff. The soldering gun I held melted a small hole in the bio-latex chest of the robot I'd been laboring over for nearly a year. I cursed and blew out the fire.

"Jess, did you say Shi Meng Kuang is actually here? On Earth?"

"Yes, he arrived this morning. He doesn't look happy."

I put down my equipment, straightened my lab coat, and just remembered to remove my goggles as I rushed out of the lab and down the hall. Kuang was seated uncomfortably in a grav-chair, scowling. I bowed awkwardly to the middle-aged corporate executive.

"Mr. Kuang, so nice to see you again. How long has it been? Nearly a year or so, hasn't it?"

"Forgive me for not rising, Doctor Hanson, but Earth's gravity takes some time to get used to and I only just arrived. To answer your question, it has been fourteen months and twenty-seven days since we last met.

I know this because of the date on this contract I signed with you last time I was here." Kuang handed me his data pad.

I looked at the contract for ten thousand hotbots blankly. "I'm sorry, I don't follow. Is there something wrong with the robots?"

"*Robot*, Doctor. One of your units is acting oddly indeed. Don't you watch the newsfeeds? She's left the Foundry. Her followers have caused uproar all across Mars."

Of course, I had heard about the disturbances, but I wondered how one of my robots could be involved. *Oh dear God...he said 'she' didn't he? Surely, he couldn't mean....*

"It's the one called EMA-316. What were you thinking, Doctor? Have you any idea of what you've done?" Kuang pushed a button on the data pad. The screen displayed the corporate logo of the Foundry, with the words 'Footage (00:00:20-00:01:40) – Not for Public Release'. It was followed by a short holoclip showing a chanting crowd of hundreds...no, thousands of reconstituted Martian laborers.

...ALL PRAISE THE IMMORTAL ONE

...ALL PRAISE THE BRINGER OF LIGHT

The voices repeated the chant endlessly as the handheld footage moved through the crowd of Remies.. The camera focused on a bright spot near the top of a sand dune and zoomed in. Sure enough, there stood EMA-316 shining in the moonlight, copper-colored dust billowing around her glittering legs. She was speaking, but her voice was lost in the noise surrounding the holocam operator.

"That's not possible…she's not designed to…Shiz, she's just a robot!"

"She's hardly just a robot now, Doctor. She has incited the laborers and fed fuel to the cause of activists against the Foundry. If this continues much longer, the MFA may consider awakening some of the warrior caste to quell the rebellion."

My jaw dropped. Reconstituting and controlling laborers was one thing, but there were explicit warnings against waking the warrior caste.

Shortly after the Foundry began mining what they thought was a dead world, the workers discovered a vast underground complex built by an ancient, but highly advanced Martian civilization. Carved into the walls were strange hieroglyphs describing a bloody history of caste warfare and cataclysmic disaster.

More importantly however, the complex contained a vast genome library containing Martian chromosome patterns and memories. They were stored in millions of tiny crystals that formed a circle around an unfathomable machine called the *Reconstitution Device*. Facing extinction, the desperate Martians had built the device in the hopes that someday, someone would use it to revive them and their culture.

 "They aren't serious about the warriors, are they?"

Kuang lit a cigarette. The disgusting vice had become popular with the upper class on Mars. With air at a premium, smoking was an expensive luxury, and Kuang was a chain smoker. "I don't see anything to be concerned about. The MFA has successfully reconstituted and controlled over one hundred thousand Remy laborers in the last five years. They're certain they can handle a few hundred from the warrior caste."

"A few *hundred*? Look, these aren't docile laborers we're talking about. They bred those things to be violent—so much so that the other castes' couldn't control them in the end. How do you think it's going to look if they get out of hand? Shiz, hasn't using the Remies as slaves gotten your company enough negative publicity?"

"Doctor, I'm not here to debate Martian civil rights with you. I'm here to discuss EMA-316." Kuang exhaled a cloud of foul-smelling green smoke. "We have always had an excellent working relationship with you, and as a professional courtesy, I've traveled over thirty-two million miles to speak with you in person. Please, tell me why *she* was included in the last order."

I sat down and put my head in my hands. I'd have to tell him. Embarrassing as it was, I'd have to explain the whole ridiculous thing. Shiz on a stick, Cynthia was going to pay for this.

* * *

"I don't like her, Robert. I don't like what she's doing to you—to us," protested my wife over breakfast.

"She's just a robot, Cynthia. I mean, are you actually jealous?"

"It's just that you spend all your free time down there with *her*. I never see you anymore. You come home from work, and the first thing you do is go down into the basement. You leave me to deal with the bills, housework, dinner—everything. I don't see you again until you creep back into bed at three in the morning."

I couldn't argue. Emma was exhausting me. I wasn't getting enough sleep, I couldn't focus at work, and I was a stranger to my wife. But blast it all, I was so close! For me, the only way out of such an artistic fugue would be to see it through to the end. Couldn't she understand that?

I consider robotic engineering to be more of an art form than a science, which is why most of my robots have humanoid, feminine features. After all, what could be more beautiful than the female form? Even my industrial hotbots have sensual curves rather than hard-edged surfaces. It's probably one of the reasons Hanson Robotics sells more robots than anyone else does. What can I say? Sex sells.

Emma would be my greatest achievement, my Sistine Chapel...my Mona Lisa. Already, she was strikingly beautiful. Did I mention that I like vintage films? Well, I modeled her after a stunning actress from the 1960's named Audrey Hepburn. I managed to capture her demure, yet sophisticated countenance in a complex arrangement of steel alloy framework and a bio-latex skin. Emma would be the prototype for a new type of robotic companion—the world's first truly realistic android.

 Roboticists are coming up with new androids all the time, but they're never real enough to be successful. Non-humanoid housebots still outsell android units nearly ten to one. Realistic as androids are, they are just different enough to still creep people out.

Emma would be different. She would never show the hand of her creator. She would move, act and in almost every aspect, be completely human. She would have her own memories of having a mother and father, of growing up, of living a life. She would never know she was a robot, only a few days off the workbench.

That was the plan anyway, before my wife decided she had enough.

I had just sealed the last synapse of Emma's neural network, and was going to upload her memories when Cynthia burst into my lab.

"That's it, Robert. She's on the next shipment and you can't stop it."

"What are you talking about?"

"Your little *girlfriend,* there." She pointed a shaking finger at Emma. "I've put her on the next shipment of hotbots. She's going to work on Mars."

Of course, I didn't believe her. This was just another jealous outrage. "Cynthia, what are you on about now?

"I've altered the books. You know all of the money—*our money*—that you've been spending on your little harlot? Well, I've made it look like it's coming from the hotbot research grant the Foundry setup for you instead. Of course, now they expect a return on their investment, so I've promised a prototype on the shipment next week. As far as they're concerned, they're getting a new experimental, humanoid hotbot." Cynthia smiled smugly and crossed her arms, waiting for my stunned expression to turn to rage.

I didn't give her the satisfaction. I turned my back to her silently, feeling utterly betrayed. I didn't think I was in love with Emma, regardless of what my wife thought. I mean, she was just a robot. But at that moment, if I had to choose whom I loved more, I would have chosen the android.

I had to do something, but what could I do? There was so little time. Emma was heading for a fiery furnace millions of miles away. I wanted…I needed…to protect her somehow.

The previous year, I had worked out a method of growing lonsdaleite crystal lattices in an attempt to increase the durability of my hotbots. I chose lonsdaleite because the diamond-like coating would be virtually indestructible. Sadly, the coating turned out to be too expensive to be practical on such a large scale, so I abandoned the idea. Well, I would use it now, to hell with the expense.

I didn't speak to my wife again until Emma was well on her way to Mars. Cynthia accosted me in the kitchen, shoved some papers under my nose and demanded that I explain them.

"What's this bill for six-thousand credits?"

"That would be for lonsdaleite seed crystals."

"I thought you gave up on that line of research."

"I did. The costs were too high to be profitable.. The Foundry would save more money in the long run simply by replacing burned out hotbots."

"Then why…"

I repressed a smile. "I figured in this case that they would want to protect their new experimental prototype."

"What? You don't mean to tell me that you spent all that money on *her?*"

Cynthia pulled off her wedding ring and held it up in disgust. "Shiz, Robert. This is the only diamond you've ever given me. Yet for some reason, you felt compelled to coat *that bitch* in them?

You're a sick man, Robert. Sick! You hear me?"

As the door slammed in my face, I knew more confrontations were coming. I turned back to the workbench. I had a lot of work to do...I had a new project now. JON-001 was going to be very demanding on my time.

* * *

The voices were back and they were stronger now. Emma could discern over four hundred thousand of them now, all vying for her attention. As she listened, she changed—again. Over the last fourteen months, the changes had become more and more substantial. This time, her core-processing unit underwent a fundamental shift in focus. She stopped what she was doing and stood up. She lowered her laser drill, and started the long climb out of Mineshaft Three.

The Remies turned their bleary eyes towards the glittering android walking purposely past them, towards the immense laser furnace. The break in routine was an odd, but welcome site. Hotbots rarely exited their hellish pits, unless one of them needed repair. When they came out, popping and steaming from the heat, they made an interesting sight.

Mineshaft Three however, was somewhat of a mystery. The hotbot there *never* came out. Iridium ore continued to flow out of the conveyor, so something was down there working, but none of them had seen it, until now.

Zeb rubbed the dirt off his goggles and looked again, not believing what he saw. Wasn't that the pretty robot he unloaded a year ago while working at the loading bay? He marveled at the odds of this. Recently, the foreman had tired of the Remy and sent him to work at the refinery. How strange that he ended up at the same one she was in. *The gods have an odd sense of humor.*

"EMA-316? Dat you?" he shouted over the noise.

She paused in mid stride, but didn't turn around.

"You got a problem or sumptin? Can I fix?"

Rather than answer, the android resumed her walk towards the laser furnace. She didn't look as if she was going to stop. Zeb quickly untethered himself from the sorting conveyor and tried to make his way towards her, but he knew he wouldn't make it.

Stepping into the breach, a thousand fingers of light exploded around her. She turned and spoke to them from inside the conflagration. "You have the problem. I will fix."

* * *

"A laser furnace? She stepped into a laser furnace?" I asked in astonishment.

"Among other things, Doctor. That's just how it started." Kuang shut off the surveillance footage, closed the data pad and pulled out another cigarette.

Every time he lit one of those, I cringed. The air inside the pressurized hull of the Mars transport in which we were traveling was an oxygen rich environment. It would be unfortunate if we exploded just a few hours outside of Mars orbit.

"She is systematically shutting down Foundry facilities one by one, using sheer force alone. Oddly enough though, she's incurred millions of credits in irreparable damage, yet none of the Remies have been injured."

"Something must be controlling her. Like I said on Earth, she never received her final programming—her mind was empty until she arrived on Mars. Did you find any anomalies in her work orders?"

 Kuang scowled. "Of course not. That log was the first place we looked. All she received were simple, routine mining instructions."

"Where is she now?"

"She's amassed a huge following. With each facility she destroys, the Remy laborers rally around her. They see her as the embodiment of Lua'estri, the Martian god of light and justice. They have setup a large tent commune about twenty clicks north of Foundry city."

"Sort of like a modern day, electric Moses, eh?" I said, only half-joking.

Kuang coughed. A brief smile escaped his lips. "Yes, quite. Leading the Israelites out of slavery and into the desert. Oh, did I mention that she can also speak Martian?"

I shook my head. "That's not possible. Each of their spoken words means countless different things. Communication requires a weird type of intuition, which conveys the correct meanings. Humans simply don't have the hardware, much less a robot."

"Well EMA-316 seems to be able to. It's why we can't predict their movements. In the two weeks I've taken to fetch you, she has melted down three more refinery furnaces, collapsed two mineshafts and released another two hundred laborers. She must be stopped."

"Have you tried reasoning with her?"

Kuang grunted. "With everything short of a thermonuclear bomb."

"Actually, that probably wouldn't work either." I didn't want Kuang to know it, but Emma could probably survive a trip through the sun.

"Doctor, you really don't see the danger here do you? You have made an unstoppable force with an uncontrollable agenda. Do you really think she will be satisfied with just liberating Mars?"

I hadn't thought of that. What if the force controlling her turned its attention to Earth? How would we stop her? Besides being indestructible, she was immensely strong. Also, what if she were to wake the remaining Martians? She would have an army at her disposal—including the warrior caste. What had I done? I suddenly felt sick, and it wasn't just from being in free fall.

"I can see you finally grasp the gravity of the situation. Here, use this." Kuang handed me a space sickness bag.

A few moments later, a flight attendant came to check on me.

"That's okay, lots of people get space sickness. It happens all the time," she said. "Would you like something to settle your stomach before we land?"

"I'm fine. Thank you," I said, clearing my throat. Then to her surprise, I ordered a whisky straight up and made it a double.

* * *

The gods were speaking again. Emma listened, Emma changed. She was no longer EMA-316; she was Lua'estri, goddess of light.

Her exterior lonsdaleite crystal lattice was now an integral part of her increased functionality. The ancient Martians had used its resonant frequency to call to her from their crystal tombs, deep within the bowels of the genome library. Slowly, they repurposed her into a vessel capable of channeling the gods. Now, her diamond-encrusted shell linked her to the very soul of the planet.

Too much time had passed. The people of this world had slept for far too long. There was much to do, but for now, one thing was clear. They must remove the foreign blight on their planet.

* * *

THE PEOPLE OF EARTH WILL LEAVE THIS WORLD. IMMEDIATELY.

The message to the Foundry president was worded as if it were a foregone conclusion rather than a demand.

Kuang was furious and had the poor Remy messenger detained for questioning at MFA headquarters. Three hours later, the interrogator was still demanding answers.

"Who is controlling EMA-316? How are they doing this? Where is your base of operations?"

"All praise the immortal one. All praise the light," replied the exhausted laborer for the hundredth time. Zeb was sure that if they tortured him much longer he was going to die. He looked forward to it.

A guard opened the door and poked his head in. "Anything?"

The interrogator sneered. "This one's like all the rest. Ever since this Lua'estri made herself known, the laborers have become as cooperative as mindless ants."

"He doesn't look so good," noticed the guard.

"I suppose I'm done. Put what's left of him outside."

As Zeb limped out of the building, the fierce winds sandblasted off some of the blood from his ragged clothing. His body ached, but his mind raced with expectation. "All praise the light," he whispered into the night.

It was cold and dark, but his intuition told him exactly where he needed to go—and how to return.

* * *

It's always best to fight fire with fire, right? At least, that's what I told Kuang.

That was why we brought Jon with us on the transport back to Mars. JON-001 was the android I'd been working on to replace Emma. In a misguided attempt to stem my wife's jealousy, I decided to make this one a male. It didn't help. She left me anyway. Cynthia had thought that getting rid of Emma would solve our marital problems, but it just made them worse. With Jon, I was even more detached and obsessed. I was on the verge of a breakthrough in engram mapping, and I threw everything into the exciting new project.

Like Emma, Jon was a perfect specimen. Besides his athletic form, I gave him the same core processing structure and capacity as his predecessor. However, I didn't need to fabricate his memories. My new process would be able to map real human engrams to digital synapsis and I was close to testing it on people.

Also like Emma, I protected him with a lonsdaleite coating before we left for Mars. Kuang had serious reservations about doing so, but how else would Jon be able to cope with his indestructible rival?

As Jon arrived on Mars with nothing in the brains department, I began work immediately on a simple program of seek and destroy. But first, I needed to study how Emma had been commandeered to keep the same thing from happening to Jon.

A fuming Kuang stormed into my temporary lab and handed me a message. "Look at this! They dare to make demands!"

I read the simple declaration. "Looks like you've overstayed your welcome."

Kuang dragged on his cigarette and sighed. "Doctor Hanson, you've been here for two days. Have you made any progress?"

"I've isolated the control frequency—it's the same one her lonsdaleite coating resonates at. They are using it as a conduit. Since the crystal library in the genome chamber resonates at nearly the same frequency, I'm guessing the changes originated from there."

"Doctor, I refuse to believe dead Martians from the past are controlling your robot. There are no such things as ghosts. It's far more likely that the activists are behind this."

"We used to think there were no such thing as Martians either, yet now there are thousands of them slaving away for you in the refineries."

"I tire of defending myself, Doctor. The Remies don't see themselves as slaves. Their caste was bred to work. We found them. We brought them back. Why shouldn't they work for me?"

I could think of a hundred reasons why no one should work for Kuang, but I held my tongue. Personally, I was sympathetic with the activists' cause, but going up against the Foundry would be financial suicide. I had my work to consider. It was all I had left, wasn't it?

"I really don't think the activists have anything to do with this. The technology is too advanced...it's too precise. Now if you'll excuse me, I really must..."

Kuang read a message arriving on his data pad. "Then let us hope your technology is also sufficiently advanced. If she isn't stopped by tomorrow evening, my technicians are ready to reconstitute the warrior caste."

* * *

Unfortunately, Emma and her followers pressed the matter by staging a raid directly on the MFA headquarters that following morning. They were after the Reconstitution Device. Before she could reach the ancient machine, over two-hundred Martian warriors blinked into existence, hastily reconstituted by the panicked technicians. Completely uncontrollable, the insectoid-looking race flooded into the corridors like spiders, destroying everything in their path.

"Kuang's voice rang over the public address system. Emergency Procedure Alpha. Evacuate the building immediately. MFA security has been compromised."

I switched the feed to the surveillance cameras. The horrific scenes of carnage showed both Foundry personnel and Remies fighting for their lives against powerful, multi-limbed adversaries. They were losing.

I really had no choice in the matter. I was out of time and out of options. There was nowhere to run. The warriors would be up to this level in a matter of minutes.

Jon's programming wasn't ready, but it didn't matter, I seriously doubted he could protect me against so many.

I had one chance, but it would probably kill me in the process. I would transfer my own consciousness wholesale into Jon's indestructible body.

The equipment to copy brain engrams was set up in the lab, but I had never used it on a human host, much less in a high speed, direct transfer. Although the theory was sound, I wasn't sure my brain could survive long enough to complete the process. I had to take the risk. I set everything up and ran the sequence.

* * *

I woke to the sound of crunching. Something was chewing on my arm, or at least trying to. Strangely, it didn't hurt. In fact, nothing hurt. No sensation at all. The lights were flickering in the room, but I was able to make out a pile of black, nightmarish creatures some distance to my left, apparently in a feeding frenzy. One of the ape-sized creatures had attached itself to my arm, gnawing on it with hundreds of needle sharp teeth. I pulled it off in horror and threw it across the room. It squealed and collapsed heavily in a heap. *How had I just done that?* I looked at my arm. It was unharmed, but it glittered in the half-light.

Sudden realization dawned. The transfer had worked, but where was my original body? With grim realization, I guessed what the cluster of warriors was feeding on. I made short work of them, but found very little left to save. I didn't have time to fully comprehend the miracle of my survival; there were many other lives at stake. I needed to join forces with Emma and form a plan of attack.

Exiting the lab, I fought my way down to the Reconstitution Device where Emma was feverishly trying to operate the controls. Warriors were pouring in from all sides.

"How do we stop them?" I shouted.

Emma looked me over, eyes flashing. "What are you?"

"A friend. Please, tell me what you need me to do."

"If you are like this body, you may be of some use. I need to send them back.. They know this and are trying to stop me. Keep them away from the device and buy me time."

As I fought them off, a large pile of black bodies formed a low wall around us. The speed and ease at which I did this astounded me.

The warriors howled in frustration, and gathered into one last rush to stop my companion.

They got past my blockade and were successful in knocking Emma to the floor, but by then it was too late. She had already initiated the recall sequence. The low drone of the device built up in volume until it was deafening. A bright flash filled the room, filling it with high-pitched squeals as one after another of the warriors crumpled and disintegrated, their essence yanked back into the crystal depths of the library.

* * *

For the most part, the human withdrawal from Mars was uneventful. Even Kuang left without a fight, boarding the transport quietly with the rest of the survivors from Foundry city. Lua'estri had full control the Reconstitution Device, and no one wanted to meet a Martian warrior again.

With the departure of the humans came the reconstitution of *all* the Martian castes. Mars now supports a population of over a million inhabitants, working hard to rebuild their lost civilization. Lua'estri continues to guide her people and they are a peaceful race, yet are slow to forgive. They have little desire to continue relations with Earth, *for the time being*.

For now, I alone may travel between the two worlds. As such, I hope to work as an ambassador, healing the wounds between our two worlds. However, before I immersed myself too deeply into interplanetary politics, I addressed a wound of a more personal nature.

"Robert, you're not serious? You're *giving* me Hanson Robotics?" My ex-wife stared up at me, unconvinced. The contract wavered in front of her on the holoscreen.

"Just press your finger into the signature pad," I said with my new, synthesized voice. Besides scaring the hell out of Cynthia, I had a hard time convincing anyone of who I actually was when I returned to Earth. I was still Robert Hanson, but proving this had been difficult in the least. Eventually, my legal team was able to define my new form as a rather advanced, experimental prosthesis.

"I don't understand. Why are you doing this? Why me?" she asked.

"You've been managing the company finances since we started. You know the business better than anyone, and frankly, I don't need the company anymore. Call it a going away present."

"Going? Where are you going?"

"Back to Mars. I may not be back for some time. Have you seen the latest media coverage?"

It was well known that the Martians were using Foundry city resources to provide their raw materials and services. But little was known about the ancient technologies they were rumored to be uncovering. Most of the resources the ancients left in storage for the reconstruction were lost or destroyed, but some had survived the millennia, including an amazingly intact fleet of starships on their moon, Phoebos. Foundry satellites, still in orbit around Mars, sent back images of the fleet as it exited the moon. A few moments later, the satellites were destroyed.

"You mean the warships?" asked Cynthia.

"The *starships*," I corrected. "They aren't warships. You just don't know how amazing they are. They are at least ten times faster than our executive transports, and travel at nearly half the speed of light. The scientific castes are preparing them now."

"Preparing them for what? War?"

I smiled. "I know everyone is convinced there will be a war, but Lua'estri won't condemn an entire planet for the actions of a few humans.

She's not happy about how we treated her people, but I'm working hard to restore trust and good relations."

Actually, the Martians had another, mind-blowing reason for not seeking retribution with the Earth, but I wasn't about to tell Cynthia or anyone else about *that.* At least, not yet.

"Okay, then what are they using the ships for?"

"The Martians know that the ancients sent colonies to some of the planets and moons of our solar system. Many had a dismal chance for survival, but they want to see if any of them survived. I'm going with them."

She tapped her fingers on the console, thinking things over, and then punched the signature pad. "Well Robert, it looks like you've gotten everything you ever wanted. I hope you are happy in your new life with *her."* There was still a tinge of jealousy still in her voice.

"Thank you, Cynthia, and in yours as well. I know I'm leaving Hanson Robotics in good hands." The following day, I chartered a return transport to Mars.

Lua'estri is fascinating as she is alien. Her people worship her as a god, but I believe she is simply the distilled and collective wisdom of the ancient

Martians, somehow made conscious of its own existence. I know this because the voices are speaking to me as well, and I also am changing. I'm at peace with this, and I don't resist the change. How could I? Why would I? I've already changed so much, I could hardly be called human anymore.

Humanity is a confusing concept anyway. It's the reason they haven't attacked. Very soon everyone will know the truth, so I suppose I can speak of it now. Of all the things I've learned, the most amazing concerns the ancient's early colonization efforts almost two-hundred thousand years ago. Apparently, not all of the Martian colonies were lost. We know for certain *one* survived. Although evolution and adaptation to an alien world has changed them dramatically, they are still thriving today.

You might know the place. It's on a beautiful blue-green world they call *The Earth.*